Escape From Marcy

Leon Thomas

This is a work of fiction. Names, characters, places and incidents either are the production of the author's imagination or are used fictitiously. Any resemblance to events or persons, living or dead, is entirely coincidental.

This book or any portion thereof may not be reproduced or used in any manner whatsoever without the express written permission of the publisher except for the use of brief quotations in a book review.

To contact the author: LThomas1128@hotmail.com

To my parents

When we have lost everything, including hope, life becomes a disgrace and death a duty. — Voltaire (1694-1778)

Poverty is the mother of crime. — Marcus Aurelius (121 -189AD)

Make sure you can rap, in case your degree doesn't work out. — KRS-One

CONTENTS

CHAPTER ONE

Marcus awakened just in time to slip through the closing door. It was Flushing Avenue and he had almost missed his stop. He took a deep breath, surveyed the area for a minute and made his way down the stairs of the subway station and walked into the sunny streets of Bedford Stuyvesant. He threw his backpack over his shoulders, adjusted his baseball cap, walked west on Flushing Avenue and continued onward towards Marcy Avenue.

As he headed west, he recalled over hearing conversations from prison guards and inmates at the penitentiary regarding the neighborhood he was about to enter. He was told that the neighborhood had become infested with a substance more valuable than gold.

A new president had stepped into power a few months earlier, promising to ebb the epidemic that had been plaguing the inner cities. Having eight years of experience as vice president of the United States under his belt, the president had not produced the results that the community had hope for when he was inaugurated into office. The epidemic had gotten worst and had become an intricate part of everyone's life in the housing projects. Marcus had just walked into the height of an epidemic that was being fueled by a substance that users called crack cocaine. It possessed and commanded all facets of the user's life; to the users of it, crack cocaine had become a deity. The epidemic, like a cancer, had spread deep into the civilian population of the Brooklyn ghettos with Marcy Houses has its capital.

Marcus was of medium height, an average built with dark hair and sharp features. He was dark in complexion and like to wear his hair short, he wasn't ugly; he was just a perfectly ordinary looking guy.

As he approached the housing units on Flushing Avenue, he could see young men, some wearing wife beaters and du-rags, assembled near the corner deli looking cautiously at each car that drove through the city streets. Young girls were seen strolling pass the young men, pushing baby strollers and wearing seductive clad clothing bearing it, for all to see.

Each day at the crack of dawn, one would find these same young men positioned, like soldiers on a battlefield, attending their post, selling to residents and passerby, a substance that would prevent them from seeing the abyss that permeated their reality.

Marcus continued to walk, slowly, along the jagged and worn down concrete sidewalk looking for any changes in the general appearance of the community since his departure. From what he saw it wasn't an issue of what had changed but an issue of what hadn't changed.

Plastic soda bottles and empty potato chip bags concealed parts of the sidewalks. The burnt out patches of brown grass throughout the landscape and the uncultivated flower gardens along the corner of the buildings reminded Marcus of the neglect and deterioration that the housing project had been dealing with for years.

He faced the entrance of the building and took a deep

breath. There were a few young men waiting outside, near the entrance, who gave him a look of someone that was of an unfamiliar face. He gave them a series of non-threatening gestures; he nodded at each one of them and awkwardly removed his cap momentarily. He then opened the main door and looked inside before walking in; it was a habit he had developed that was still ingrained within him even though he had not been home in years. He walked inside and was not too surprised but was a little amazed at the nauseating odor and scenery which he encountered. He gave off a deep sigh and stared at the graffiti that plagued the walls. The hallway leading to the elevator was littered with old newspapers, candy wrappers, cigarette butts, condoms and something he was not used to seeing. It was crack vials; they were everywhere on the floor and on the stairs. They littered the place like broken sea shells on a beach.

Marcus made his way pass the elevator and up the stairs, avoiding the elevator for now, not knowing what he would witness. The building was eerily silent as most people slept during the day and came out of their dwellings like vermin after sundown.

When he reached the second floor to his surprise and disbelief, was a man in his forties lying on the floor half naked, passed out on his stomach. His head slightly turned just enough to the left so his eye lids could be seen flickering through the dim sunlight, that escaped through the opened window. A used crack pipe could be seen beside his lifeless body near his half open mouth. Marcus walked passed him and continued further, little more than halfway up the flight of stairs to the third floor where he could see the apartment. He paused on the end of the landing and gazed at the door with the number on it. He could smell food coming from behind the door; he knocked on the gray wooden door three times and

3

waited after taking a deep breath.

An untidy, elderly woman in a white cotton gown, wearing an apron embroidered with oranges and apples opened the door. A long pause engulfed the two of them; they stared at each other. The elderly woman was able to break her silence and spoke with a feeling of both grief and happiness.

"My lord, Jesus, my son has returned home," the woman said wiping her hands on her apron.

Before Marcus could say a word, the woman threw her arms around him and hugged him tightly.

"I don't know what to say," Marcus said. "But I am glad to be home."

"Com'on in, son," the woman said gazing in awe at her son who she hasn't seen in years. "You've grown so…you a man now."

Marcus slowly walked into the living room and looked about the apartment. The furniture was old and worn, but the place was generally clean.

The smell of fried chicken and sweet corn revived his appetite. It's been years since he ate real food.

"I see they moved you to a smaller place," Marcus looked around the apartment regretfully.

"Yes, ever since you left."

"Mom, I haven't eaten real food in…"

"Well, from now on, you won't have to worry about that," his mother interrupted as she walked back to the kitchen to where the food was waiting on the stove. "I didn't know what time you would arrive," his mother said. "But it seem like I finished just in the nick of time."

Marcus looked at his mother as she moved efficiently around the kitchen, her gown and her apron moved, ruffling as she moved between the old stove and the eating table holding a pan of fried chicken and then a pot of peas and rice. Watching her move about, made him feel uncomfortable and guilt-ridden; after all he put her through, he was surprised at the love she still had for him. A home coming meal was what she prepared for him; he felt undeserving of it. Seeing her at work brought flashbacks of her preparing breakfast for him and his older brother, during the time his brother started going to high school before he was killed.

Marcus was given a plate of what was a complete contrast to what he have been used to in the past few years of his life. The more he smelled that aroma of the food the more he remembered how bad things were for him and what he had been missing. Food was not the only thing that was missing from him. Marcus missed seeing his former girlfriend and his daughter. His girlfriend was pregnant when he last seen her. He only saw his daughter once when she came to visit him in prison with her mother.

The fact that his daughter is being raised without a father made him more concerned about her welfare. While in prison, he spent quite a number of hours at the prison library learning as much as he could. He read about how the system set up traps to incarcerate young black men. He knew that it would be hard for him to find work with a felony, which meant he would have to avoid the temptation of the underworld to make money. Going back to the joint was not an option for him. However, it may very well be the only road that is available to him; he must create a new road for himself if he is to survive in the Brooklyn ghetto.

"You know Ma," Marcus said. "When I walked up the stairs to come here, there was a half-naked man lying out cold on the staircase on the second floor."

"Oh, get use to it," his mother said. "In the past four years, things around here have gotten worst. They smoke that crap in the elevator, on the stairs, in the playground, you name it…I've never seen things this bad before."

"I have to admit, I was caught a little of guard."

"So, what are you planning to do with yourself?" his mother said sitting at the kitchen table holding a cob of corn.

"I don't know, Ma," Marcus looked up at her. "I really don't know."

"Well you gotta do something, boy," his mother said. "A real man makes his own money."

"I was thinking about cutting hair," Marcus said chewing food in his mouth.

"How long will it take you to get a clientele?"

"A couple of weeks…maybe months," Marcus said. "I still would need money to get started."

"Would you need money to get a certificate?"

"Yeah, that too."

The two finished and got up from the table and placed the dirty dishes in the sink.

"There's a mail for you on the table, ya see it?" his mother asked, walking to the bathroom.

Marcus turned to see a brown envelope on the table in the living room section of the apartment, from the Kings County Family Court. It was a subpoena to appear in court, regarding child support. He'd just got home and the last thing he needed was stress. He threw the envelope on the table and walked over to the sofa in the living room. The smell of the old sofa scratched his sinuses. The brown sofa was half worn, and torn from constant wear and tear as it stood out in the open. Marcus sat on the sofa and contemplated what he needed to do, and what his next move would be. He thought about his daughter, which he hadn't seen in over a decade. After what he saw, so far coming home, he was appalled to even image what influences his daughter might have been subjected to while he was in jail. He would have to make amends with his daughter's mother. He felt that he needed to be a part of her life if he was to end the vicious cycle that was crippling his generation and eventually his daughter's.

It was the next morning, and Marcus had gotten dress and decided to head on out to the only barber shop he knew since he was a child. He was in great need of a haircut as he noticed from looking through the bathroom mirror while washing up. After breakfast he made his way down the staircase and out through the front door.

It was early summer, and the sun had risen across the cloudy gray and morning sky. Suddenly, a strong beam of sunlight broke through the heavily overcast sky, hitting Marcus in the face as he cast his eyes upward. The strong beam piercing the clouds overhead had burnt away a section of the gray clouds, allowing the rays of the sun to cast its influence over the community of Bedford-Stuyvesant. He walked briskly and erectly, as he continued on Myrtle Avenue towards Marcus Garvey Blvd. He walked down Marcus Garvey Blvd avoiding pedestrians going to work and waiting at the corner for a bus.

He viewed the old barber shop from across the street. It looked the same since the last time he had an afro there almost fourteen long years ago. The shop was smack in the middle of the block next door between a diner and a small beauty supply store that conveniently sold barber supplies. The old sign which read *Doc's Snip & Cut Barber Shop* hung loosely over the store's front entrance. The metal door had been partially ripped from its frame and the front windows have been naturally tinted by dust particles from years of neglect.

Marcus opened the half broken door and looked inside. Two familiar faces became apparent. Doc, the owner of the barber shop, had a customer in his chair. His station was the closest to the door. The barber shop had two customers sitting on a fake leather sofa waiting to be served; an old gentleman reading a newspaper and a younger gentleman who was wearing headphones and a Walkman at his side.

Marcus noticed a childhood friend who noticed him after a long stare. He didn't expect to see him there at the exact same spot fourteen years later; he thought his friend would have moved on by now. His friend was sitting on the barber's chair, while waiting for clients. When he walked further in, he smelt the scent of burning cigarettes; however no one was smoking at the time.

"Marcus!" a voice was heard as his friend jumped up from the barber's seat to greet him.

"Carter," Marcus embraced his long-time friend. "It's been a while, man."

"Where you been?"

Marcus stepped back holding his chin and gazed at Carter who was surprised to see him. "I've been in the joint, for quite some time."

Carter was light-skinned, of medium height and wore a flat-top haircut. His thin frame fitted nicely in his small barber's jacket.

"So I see you still here," Marcus said in a melancholy voice. "I thought you were going back to school an' shit."

Carter rubbed the back of his head while looking down and didn't answer. "You here for a cut?" Carter asked as he gestured his chin towards the barber's chair.

Marcus walked over and sat down and made himself comfortable in the chair.

"What you been up to?" Carter asked adjusting the electric razor.

"Just trying to get back in the swing of things," Marcus said. "I'm going to need a job soon; I'm broke as a bat. What job is out there for a felon?"

"Well," Carter laughed. "What I'm going right now, I guess."

"How's that working out for ya?"

"I'm still in the hood," Carter answered. "For some reason I can't escape outta this bitch for nothin'. How you plan to escape the hood?"

"Man, my daughter's mother been hounding me for child support, even when I was in the joint; and I know she gon' becoming after me soon enough."

"Most niggas around here got the same problem, bro, it ain't just you."

"Man…how can I pay child support when I don't have a fucking job?"

"Turn your head a little bit to the right, I am almost done," Carter moved his friend's head slightly and passed the razor over the side of his head.

"Don't forget to spray alcohol when you're done."

"How was she supporting your kid, when you were in the joint?"

"Section 8 housing, she's in the projects, I guess, I don't fucking know," Marcus said in a frustrating voice slamming his fist against the armrest.

"When you going see her?"

"Who?"

"Your daughter."

"I'm gona go see her tomorrow. I need to see my daughter, that all I know."

"How you and her mother broke apart?"

"You know, we were just kicking it, nothing serious at least, at least in the beginning. I wanted to leave the relationship you know. She, I guess felt that I was just using her for sex. She is a hood rat, fucking hood rat."

"How she got pregnant," Carter asked as he finished

lining up the sides of his head.

Marcus became uncomfortable as he realized that the other people in the shop had taken an interest in what he was saying. Although some were pretending to be preoccupied with reading newspapers and engaging with other matters, he knew that he was becoming the center of attention and it made him quite uncomfortable.

"Carter, you know what," Marcus replied. "I remember that day when she invited me over after we had that argument, and I had told her that I wasn't interested in seeing her again. It was almost three weeks since the last time that argument happened, and I hadn't seen her since. She called me, telling me that she needed to see me an' shit. Something told me not to go, but I went."

"Close your eyes," Carter interrupted as he sprayed alcohol on Marcus' fresh cut hair.

"When I got there," Marcus continued. "She was so much different than before. She was all nice and shit. She was wearing a nice tight ass dress that stopped right below her ass. Man that was the best make up sex...better yet that was the best pussy she ever gave me, man."

"I bet you didn't wear any protection that time," a customer said with a nervous laughter.

"You know what you're damn right, man. Usually, she would remind me to put on a rubber, but this time the bitch was all over my ass."

"You done," Carter said removing the cloth from his neck.

Marcus got off the chair and paid Carter twelve dollars.

"I'll be back again, man...," Marcus said. "Good to see you again, though, hopefully we can find a way and get the fuck outta da hood, for real."

"I'm sure something will come along," Carter replied as

he patted his friend on the shoulders. "The next time we see each other, who know maybe we can get something going." Carter saw his friend walking towards the door. "Oh, Marcus, I know you just got back and everything, but, do, be careful up there at Marcy. There's mad crackheads up in there, man."

An elderly man with side burns and grayed out hair sitting on the sofa, waiting to get his hair cut interrupted the conversation.

"Yeah, the shit is crazy over there," he said, still looking at the newspaper he was reading. "Ever since that shit they called crack hit the projects couple a years ago, man, niggas be walking around like zombies an' shit. My suggestion to you homey, stay clear and mine your damn business when ya there." The elderly man threw his newspaper down and looked directly at Marcus who was by the door. "With all the dope circulating up in there twenty-four seven, that place is like a damn factory now...straight up General Motors an' shit." The elderly man shook his head, laughed and continued. "By the way, stay away from them bitches up there too, fuck with 'em and you may end up losing god knows what."

"Oh yeah, like what, money?" Marcus started to laugh. "It's been a while...had to do without ass for almost fourteen years...all I had was my right hand...but I know what ya saying, pops... good looking out, though."

"One other thing," the elderly man said leaning over on the sofa. "There's only two types of people in that fucking place...actually three; the niggas who use crack, and the niggas who sell crack...and three, the niggas who are victims of the other two. Choose which category you want to be in now or the system will choose it for you later."

"Shut the fuck up," Carter said to the elderly man. "Go read your newspaper, man."

"It's aight, man," Marcus said waving his hand towards

Carter. "I survived thirteen long years in the pen; I think I can handle the hood. Besides, I've already chosen to stay outta trouble and take care of my daughter."

"Stay outta trouble?" the elderly man exclaimed wide-eyed. "Man, you sound like a damn fool."

"Shit can't be that bad," Marcus said surprised with arms stretched out.

"Let me tell you somethin'," the elderly man continued. "That place is like a fast food drive-in throughout the day and a zoo at night…"

Marcus laughed and almost fell back on the other customer getting a haircut. "This nigga is crazy," he said covering his mouth while laughing. "Yo, pops, you on medication or somethin'."

"Why you stereotyping people, man," Carter intervened. "I'm tired of your shit, old man."

"Listen, man," Marcus said. "I got to go."

"Take care," the elderly man said. "That place will have you jumping off a bridge one day, if you're not careful."

Marcus turned and started walking towards the door.

"See you soon," Carter said to him.

"Take care, my brotha," said Marcus. "I'll see you maybe in a few weeks."

Marcus left the barber shop and made his way back to the projects surveying the neighborhood like a tourist. He took the long way and went towards Myrtle & Nostrand. As he walked around the housing project, he noticed how everything changed. There were more young black men outside, mostly in wife beaters and du rags, doing nothing but pacing the area, making exchanges through car windows as cars stopped at the corner of the blocks. He was amazed at the efficiency and subtlety of how events took place in such a short period of time.

A car drove up with two sexy-clad dressed women in the back seats wearing heavy make-up and hair extensions, with and a man wearing sunglasses and a basketball jersey in the passenger seat. Out of the blue, one of the young men at the corner strolled over to the double parked car and handed the front passenger a small packet and at the same time took a folded bill from him with the same hand in one continuous movement only to return back to where he was originally standing.

Suddenly, a cold and undesirable feeling griped him as he looked around only to see the same scenario being played out elsewhere on the block; he recalled what the old man in the barber shop had told him earlier. He was seeing it for himself now, Marcy had in fact become a dope factory.

He noticed too that some of the men were flashing their jewelry as females walked by. He witness as one young man in particular, wearing a baseball cap and a pair of Jordans, purposely dropped a few bills on the ground as a female with wide hips in a tight spandex walked by him. The young man pretended and acted as if the money accidentally fell out of his pocket. From Marcus' point of view, it was three one hundred dollar bills. The female smirked and kept her head straight and walked passed him. The young man could be heard whispering under his breath saying, "Fuck that bitch."

Marcus tried to avoid any possible confrontation and struggled to stay under the radar by keeping his head down and avoiding eye contact with anyone. There was no one near the front entrance to his apartment building as he moved towards it. He looked through the front door and opened it with his key. Marcus slowly entered only to find a young lady waiting by the elevator. She was unkempt, frail, and appeared malnourished. She was wearing a thin fake leather jacket, a tight fitted skirt that exposed much of her thighs, revealing a series of tattoos. The dress had several stains that were visible because of its dark color. She wore heels that were discolored and worn due to constant wear. The blouse she wore, which was buttoned half way, barely covered her sagging breast, which exposed her left nipple. Marcus gazed at her and headed up the stairs when he heard her voice.

"Excuse me, sir," she said faintly with a touch of pity in her voice. "Can you help me?"

Marcus stretched his neck over to where the elevator is to see the young lady leaning against the elevator door.

"What do you want?" he asked.

"My kids are hungry and I need some money."

Marcus walked down the end of the steps and walked over to the elevator. He cast his eyes about and walked cautiously to avoid the various elements that were laid out on the floor that were difficult to see due to insufficient lighting.

When she smiled he noticed a front tooth was missing.

"How much do you need?"

"Ten."

"Where's your kids?"

"There upstairs in my apartment," she lied.

"With who?"

"No one, and there's no cereal, either, I need that money," she walked forward towards him very stiff and awkwardly until she got close enough. "I need to buy food for my kids."

Marcus felt unaware of himself for a moment as flashbacks of years of hard times in the penitentiary surfaced to his mind. He was intrigued by her vulnerability and her submissive behavior.

"Money is tight right now, ya know?" Marcus said as he stepped back a bit.

"I know you got cash on you," she demanded; then added

provocatively, "I suck you off for the ten."

Marcus cupped the back of his head and said, "Nah, I'm good."

"I'll swallow you for a twenty then," she replied. "Com' on nigga, I need a hit real bad or I'll go fuckin' crazy soon."

Marcus was very surprised and he tried to conceal his excitement. Blood began to flow swiftly through his veins, he felt sweat breaking out all over his body. He had never been with such a woman before. Uninhibited, unrestrained, and untamed, were the only qualities such a woman could offer him. She appealed to his lower nature. He could do to her what he couldn't do to other women that he have been or will be with, in his life, he thought to himself. She had no feelings, she was numb, and he could be unrelenting with her, he told himself. The thought aroused him; so much so she noticed the bulge in his pants. It became a struggle for him. He didn't want to get caught, and he couldn't take her into his apartment, either. It was daylight, and anyone could walk through the door at any time. He gazed at the dim light coming from the ceiling; the dark section would provide cover in case someone walked down the stairs or through the door. His eyes passed a few used condoms on the floor, which reassured him that being seen would not seem out of place by anyone in the projects.

Marcus opened his wallet and took out his last twenty dollar bill and handed it to her. "Here, take this."

She took the bill and placed it in her bosom and bottomed up her blouse.

"The elevator is broken," she said stepping back into the unlit elevator and knelled down on two sheets of newspaper that were on the floor.

Marcus looked over to the front door to see if anyone was coming in or out and proceeded to the elevator where the young lady was waiting on her knees. She quickly went for his belt and habitually unbuckled it, releasing the zipper and exposing his erected penis as she pulled his pants towards his sneakers. She took a mouth-full and began stroking it with her mouth.

She stopped momentarily after a few minutes.

"I am tried, my neck," she complained after pulling out.

"Open your fucking mouth!" Marcus demanded. Marcus grabbed her uncombed hair from the back of her head and forcefully rammed his penis down her throat causing her to gag reflex. She instinctively grabbed his shirt and tried to push his body away from her, with no results. Marcus continued to rotate his pelvis as he held her hair from the back of her head. Saliva poured from her mouth, cascading on his pants like rain falling from a window sill, as each stroke became unbearable. She began punching him wildly until he released the grip causing her head to fly back. Gasping, coughing, and holding her throat she felt a fast, sudden and sharp slap across the face which stung like a hundred mosquito bites. Before she had a chance to recover from the first one, she felt another slap across the left side of her face. She looked up at Marcus with disbelief and resentment.

"Put it back in your mouth," Marcus demanded looking down at her.

"It hurts," she whispered hold her throat with her right hand.

"Open, and put it back in your fuckin' mouth you fuckin' bitch!" he repeated his demands in an agitated voice.

She sheepishly refused.

"Suck the balls then," he added clenching his fist, which caused her to flinch.

She opened her mouth and engulfed a mouth full only to flinch and quiver at every movement of his hands. Suddenly, after a nervous twitch of her head, a cruel blow to the back of the head caused her to release her grip as saliva drooled off her lips, down to her chin and around her neck. The pain to the back of her head was enduring.

She tried to get her breath back as she absorbed the blow; she tried to form words as she anticipated another blow from him.

"Wha' cha waiting on?" Marcus asked sternly, as he clenched his fist again.

She looked up at him teary eyed and swallowed both testicles in her mouth and began moving her head back and forth. Moments later, Marcus let out a screeching sound as he fell to the floor like a sack of potatoes, holding his testicles cupped in his hand.

"Ahhh, fuck…you dumb bitch!" he screamed. "Yo, what the fuck!"

The young lady jumped on him like an alley cat as he laid on the floor in agony; she started punching him in the back of his head as he rolled over on his side, blocking series of punches with his left arm. When the front door opened, she got up, adjusted her skirt to cover her buttocks and ran pass a lady who quickly moved out of her way as she stormed out into the streets.

Marcus lay helpless, trying to come to grips with what had taken place. He looked at his fingers, checking to see if any blood was present, but could barely see through the darkness. He lay stiffened, glaring upwards, wild-eyed as he quietly groaned. After a few moments he managed to get up on his feet, adjusted his pants and made his way to the corridor.

Embarrassed and confused, he passed the lady standing at the front door who looked at him with astonishment. He held his head down and slowly climbed his way up the staircase and through his apartment, where he staggered his way to the bathroom only to collapsed on the tiled floor still holding his groin area with both hands.

"Fucking Marcy, I swear, I need to escape from this bitch," he said quietly to himself as he closed his eyes and absorbed the pain.

CHAPTER TWO

Marcus decided not to eat breakfast; he was too much in a hurry to see his daughter. He purchased two tokens from the Flushing Avenue train station token booth and walked among the crowd of people moving in and out to get to work. People on the train were reading their morning papers while others listened to their Walkmans, expressing their unpleasant faces as they awaited their destination. His baby mother lived a few blocks from the New Lots Avenue train station in East New York, Brooklyn. He started to mentally prepare himself for what was to come. He knew the type of person, Thelma was. Marcus had never cared about his daughter until now. He felt Thelma was using the system to get at him for leaving the two of them for so long.

In prison, he learned a lot from the fellas who served with him. He listened to their problems, and they listened to his. While he stood among the other passengers on the train who were pushing and shoving to get to the next available seat, he thought about how the system broke a lot of young black men. Many were serving hard times for just hanging around with the wrong type of people or being at the wrong place at the right time. He recalled a fellow prisoners who lectured him from time to time in the cell, telling him that those who were released from prison for committing a felony were no better than those who were still locked up. At least in prison, he was told, you are provided with basic care and three square meals a day; a shower, a toilet, a bed, and a warm blanket. What it didn't provide, however, was a woman, but then again there were ways for dealing with that. The system was designed to make sure you returned, though. Sure enough, it did. Marcus hoped, from the day he left the prison complex, that wouldn't be his fate.

Marcus got off the subway station and walked on Linden Blvd. He adjusted his jeans as he was still sore from yesterday's elevator encounter. He walked a few blocks and turned into the housing projects. It was quite like his, same scenario; young men patrolling the sidewalks watching cars drive by with their hands under their T-shirts. At one point he realized that he had actually passed her building. Things seemed a little different after thirteen years. When he got to the front door he rang the buzzer and was let in only to see the hallway littered with crack vials, old newspapers and roaches, engulfing the tiled floor.

He took the elevator to the fourth floor and knocked on the apartment door as his heart raced with anticipation.

A woman opened the door. Her eyes glued on his face before crossing her arms. She felt scared, yet anxious about what to expect from a man she hadn't seen in thirteen years.

"What da fuck you doing here?" Thelma said sucking her teeth.

"I came to see my daughter. Wha's up?" Marcus replied.

Marcus swallowed and looked hard at her.

"When did you come out?" she said.

"Just a few days ago."

20

Marcus couldn't help but notice Thelma's breast straining against the thin cotton T-shirt she was wearing tightly around her slim athletic frame. He slightly turned his head away as she caught him staring briefly at them, only to get caught staring again. They weren't as perky as the last time he'd seen them but they still made an impression on him. Marcus flushed but controlled himself. He noticed a vague tattoo that looked like someone's name across her chest that wasn't there before, that he couldn't make out without staring. Her curves were still all in the same places as the day he left. Her nails were long and square cut and polished, well-groomed with a French manicure. Her attitude hadn't changed though; she seemed a little bitter and salty, but he noticed she didn't slam the door in his face.

"I got your court papers in the mail when I returned home," Marcus said. "I see you didn't waste any time did you? You knew I was getting out."

"No," she replied sternly. "My lawyer did."

"Where's Keisha?" he asked sharply.

"She's inside," Thelma said turning her head towards the inside of the apartment.

As Marcus motioned to pass through the door, Thelma blocked him from passing through.

"I can't let you in," she proclaimed. "I'm having company right now."

"Can't she come to the door at least? Man it's been years."

Marcus started to become angry and frustrated, he began realizing what was beginning to happen. He knew if he pushed further, she would call the police on him. He had to make a choice; see his daughter and go to jail or let the system win.

"What the fuck is wrong with you, man," he exclaimed clenching his fist. "I just got outta da joint and you ain't gon' make me see her, are you serious."

Thelma raised her hand and pointed her finger at him and said, "You ain't seeing her. I told you, again and I'm going to say it again. I am through with you. I don't need no broke ass nigga who can't do shit for me. You can't even support yourself. Get your shit together first and then we'll talk!"

"Why you acting like this, you haven't change. Move out of the way," he said trying to push her out of the way.

"No!"

"I'm her father; don't you want what's best for our daughter?"

"She has a father already who has his own business and his own car," she said resisting his intrusion.

Marcus felt his heart skip a beat when she said that. His ego took a hit.

"What da fuck does that mean?" he asked with an emptiness that seized him.

"It means exactly what it means," Thelma said as she slowly began to close the door. "I have a boyfriend who's doing well for himself and that's her stepfather."

"Keisha," he yelled from outside the entrance to the apartment, still pushing the closing door.

"No, Keisha, don't come," Thelma said turning her head behind her, after hearing someone walking behind her from the living room. "Stay where you at."

Moments became more intense as Marcus got a glimpse of his teenage daughter who quickly moved out of sight. He felt a sweat drop trickle down his spine and he could feel more air rushing through his nose.

"Are you serious, Thelma," he shook his head in disbelief while still pushing against the door.

Marcus attempted to push his way pass the closing door. He managed to get his foot in the door, blocking it from closing. A struggle ensued. Marcus held his breath and pushed with all his might and finally got himself passed the door. Immediately, Thelma started pushing him and became hysterical. After fending off blows, Marcus walked passed a short corridor to find a young girl sitting next to a man he did not know. The girl resembled him; surely he knew who she was.

Thelma became quiet. Not knowing what to expect, she folded her arms and stared at him with disbelief and resentment. Marcus remained frozen and disoriented. Mixed feelings overwhelmed him. Rage went through his body like the ocean hitting the shore. He could hear his heart pumping, blood rushing through his veins like water rushing through a tunnel. For a split second he became dumbfounded, but managed to fight his bewilderment.

"Keisha," he said with awe to the girl on the couch.

The young girl looked at him.

"Do you know who this is?"

"Yes."

"Com' here."

Keisha got off the sofa, looked at her mother and walk over to her father. Before Marcus could hug his daughter, Thelma interrupted them.

"Keisha, go to your room."

"What," Marcus said as he touched his daughter's arm.

"Why you like this," he asked turning towards Thelma.

"I said go, Keisha."

"You know what, you are a fucking bitch," Marcus replied. "I come here after thirteen fucking years and you don't want her to see me; you jealous bitch."

"I told you, I don't need you here."

"Who's this nigga you got my daughter with," Marcus said looking at the man sitting on the couch who remained patient and calm.

Marcus couldn't help but noticed his watch as it glimmered from the sun light that passed through the window. He also noticed a thick gold chain around his neck and car keys on the center table with the initials BMW written on it. He was clean cut and wore a fresh pair of Jordans.

Seeing all of that made him furious. For a second he knew he couldn't compete with this guy and he knew he didn't have the resources to attract Thelma away from him.

"That's my boyfriend," Thelma said.

"You got him touching my daughter, yo," Marcus turned to look at Thelma.

"He ain't touching her, shut the fuck up," she yelled. "I'm calling the police."

"Call the fucking police then," he yelled back.

Marcus took a good look at the man sitting on the couch and stormed out of the apartment. He knew he had to avoid getting arrested for trespassing. He realized how little power he had over his life. The fact of not being able to see his daughter hurt him. To see another man raising his daughter made him angry. He couldn't do anything. He felt like his hands were tied.

Marcus took the elevator to the ground level and pushed the front door open as he exit the building. He had hoped for a longer visit than the one he received. He had never expected to see another man sitting there at her place. The idea of ever moving in with her was now shot down. Moving from one housing project to another was not such a great idea anyway, he thought. Marcus was hoping he could move out of the hood altogether.

For a second, as he headed back to the New Lots Avenue subway station, he realized he couldn't entirely blame Thelma for seeing someone else while he was away in prison for so long. Receiving welfare, and raising a child on public assistance, wouldn't have been enough for her to maintain her lifestyle and the wellbeing of their daughter. He had to find a way to earn a living, and get his life back together, in order to convince her that he was capable of taking care of a family. One of his goals was to win her back.

As he turned to enter the sidewalk, he quickly noticed a fairly new navy blue BMW 5 series with custom rims and an opened moon roof, parked on the street in front of the passage way leading to the building he just left. Marcus tilt his head downward and covered his face with his left hand; he couldn't help but wondered, but could only speculate who the owner of the vehicle was.

CHAPTER THREE

The next morning Marcus picked up a local newspaper from the supermarket around the corner from his building. He went straight to the help wanted ad section. He had to find work. He didn't want to cut hair for anything. That was so typical of ex-convicts. The problem with being a barber was that one had to acquire a clientele. That could take months, and he couldn't afford to wait that long. He wanted to make money right away. There were so many things he wanted to see, buy, and do. He wanted to make money without getting into trouble. He saw an ad that caught his eye. It was a custodial worker position at a well-known restaurant in the downtown Brooklyn area. Marcus had experience earning money in prison mopping the cafeteria and the restrooms. The job paid minimum wages, but it was a start, he thought. This would also give him an opportunity to gain some experience and earn some money in the meantime. He would head to the restaurant after lunch.

When Marcus walked into the restaurant, he noticed how crowded it was. There were people, literally waiting near the front entrance to be seated at a table. A young lady approached him wearing a white shirt with a fish head logo on it. She was pretty in the face, but hardly had enough in the back to hold up her pants. She looked tired, drained, and wasted. In her eyes, he could see a woman who would do anything to leave her predicament, but merely waiting for an opportunity to leave her job for something better.

"Don't block the doorway, move to the side and wait over there until you are called," she said instinctively.

"Excuse me, but I am not waiting to be seated," Marcus said to her.

"What are you hear for then?" she asked.

"I'm here about the custodian job."

"Oh, wait right here."

She left for two minutes and came back with a clipboard and pencil in hand.

"Follow me," she said as she walked to a table near the entrance to the kitchen. "Fill this out and someone will be with you shortly, okay?"

"Yes, ma'am," Marcus said grabbing the items.

The typical questions were being asked of him. He almost forgot his mother's address. He left the zip code blank, since he couldn't remember it. *Previous employment* the form stated. He thought about writing '*Hustler*', but decided to leave it blank. Suddenly his heart skipped a beat. It was the infamous question that he was warned about, regarding crime convictions. It required a yes or no answer, and an explanation. He began contemplating what he should do. Before he could get an answer a tall, slender, white man wearing glasses sat down in front of him, opposite the table.

"Finish the application?" he asked adjusting his glasses. "Oh, by the way, I'm Chuck, I'm the manager here."

"Well, I'm almost done," Marcus said.

"That's ok. Let's take a look," the manager reached out to grab the application from Marcus who nervously handed it to him.

"Do you have any experience in custodial work...Marcus?"

For a spit second, Marcus had to decide whether to mention working at the New York State Penitentiary.

"Well sir, not quite."

"Is that a yes or no?"

"No, sir."

"It says here that you live in Bedford Stuyvesant. You would have no problem commuting from there to downtown, is that correct?"

"Uh... no problem, sir, that correct."

"The hours which you would work is Monday through Thursday from 1pm to 9pm; Saturday from 2pm to 10pm. You would have Fridays and Sundays off. Would that work for you?"

"Those hours are fine."

"One other thing," the manager said as his eyes narrowed at the bottom of the page. "You left out...have you ever been convicted of a crime? We would have to do a background check for all new employees, by the way."

Marcus tried to hide his bewilderment and scratched his head. He didn't want to answer the question. He knew he couldn't lie, because a background check would expose him. Maybe they would understand his situation growing up in the hood. Everybody needs a second chance, he thought.

"Yes, sir, I have."

"You have been convicted of a crime?" the manager asked again removing his glasses.

"It was years ago. I was involved in an armed robbery... and assault, sir."

"I see, ok," the manager said with a grimace. "Well… we will process your application and if anything we will give you a call."

After the manager abruptly left, he slowly got up from the table and walked out of the restaurant feeling a sense of helplessness and discontent. Finding work was not going to be easy, he thought. Instead of taking the bus home, since he was low on money, he decided to walk east on Myrtle Avenue.

As Marcus walked up Bedford Avenue, he came across a familiar face. It was an old friend named Duncan. He hardly recognized Duncan who was wearing a dashiki and a matching hat. He had a table laid out in front of a bakery on the sidewalk. There were books, incense, necklaces, essential oils, and just about everything afrocentric on the table in front of him, with more items in a box next to the table. His demeanor was different. He seemed calm and reserved, yet studious. He had the look of despair on his eyes, though. An unkempt beard stood out on his face. Marcus found him sitting down reading a book. Duncan seemed to have traded in his leather jackets and baggy jeans for an African style pullover outfit. As Marcus walked by his table, Duncan looked up at him and instantly recognized him.

"Hotep," Duncan said getting up from the table. "Hotep!"

"Yo, man, who's this?" Marcus glanced and pretended to not recognize him.

"I see you have a bad memory."

"Yo, Duncan…long time no see you, man," Marcus said. He could smell the faint lingering odor of frankincense in the air.

"The name isn't Duncan anymore my brother. My name is Amen-Ra Ausar Neter Un."

"Amen-Ra, who?" Marcus said as he began to laugh out loud and almost bumped into a lady that walked passed him as he staggered backwards. "Man you're tripping...nigga please".

"No, I'm not...why do you say that?" Duncan seemed a little annoyed.

"I'm only messing with you man," Marcus extended his hand. "I always wondered if I'd ever see you again. You still live at Marcy?"

"I've been good, actually thing have been a little crazy for me, in the past few years, you know?"

"Like what?"

"I was in jail for a little bit."

"In jail," Marcus exclaimed. "For what?"

"When I got laid off a couple of years ago...man everything went downhill from there."

Marcus grabbed the back of his head. "You were working in the factory too, in the Bronx, I remembered."

"After my unemployment went dry...man I lost everything. I stopped paying my bills, my car notes, man you name it." Duncan turned his face away and tried to avoid looking at Marcus directly. "I ended up turning to crack...just to numb the pain, it was getting too much for me to bear. If it wasn't for the crack pipe, I'd probably would have jump off a fucking bridge by now...the pain of losing my manhood was that bad. The crack pipe saved my life, though. And to make matters worse, I ended up having to pay child support for a child that ain't even mine."

"What do you mean it ain't yours?" Marcus look surprised.

"I've only been with the bitch twice. Somebody told me she was messing around with another nigga name Chris. You see, I wasn't feeling her anymore, so I stopped seeing her. So, she lied and said I got her pregnant. I ended up going to jail for not pay child support. After that I couldn't get a job or nothing."

Marcus studied Duncan's face carefully. He found that his gaze was drawn again and again to Duncan's facial expression. Duncan's demeanor changed as he continued to tell the story of his downfall. The studious character that was portrayed when Marcus came upon him, had diminished slowly into a man who had realized that he finds himself in a world he has no control over and how he interacts within it. The façade that he wore had momentarily been exposed.

"Where did you started smoking crack?" Marcus asked.

"Marcy," Duncan said scratching the side of his face. "That place…man…Reagan fuck'd up the hood for real…man. I tell you that voodoo economic shit he talked about was bullshit…the hood never got nothin'…the money never trickled down to us. When the economy for the poor got bad and factories like mines started laying off niggas like me who live in the hood, then the crack came out of nowhere like magic, like five years ago while you was still in prison, Marcus."

Marcus was stunned and gazed motionlessly.

"Marcus, let me tell you something," Duncan said slowly and with great emotion while gazing into his friend's eyes. "Never knock a person who smokes crack. First find out the situation that brought them to that point. It's hard for some people to understand what it's like to lose everything you worked for and to be left with only your fucking shirt and two nickels to rub together. I remember the nigga who first sold me my first hit an' shit. He was a young dude who also lived at Marcy, too; maybe about thirteen or fourteen years old and shit. It was around two in the morning…the same day I got my eviction notice. I cried that night like a bitch in labor. I had given up on life; I got out of my apartment and started

31

walking to the bridge up there in Williamsburg." Duncan pointed westward and continued. "To meet my destiny with the East River, but that young nigga saved my life with a rock and a pipe. I remember…it was a hot summer night and I was walking on Nostrand all depressed and shit and he saw me, talked to me for a few minutes and sold me a hit for only five dollars, my last five dollars too… man I went back to my crib and the rest is history. After then I started stealing money from my cousin to feed my habit."

"Real talk," Marcus interrupted while his facial expression showed concern.

"I'm just keeping it real, you know," Duncan said. "Now you got this nigga George Bush talkin' all that bullshit about war on drug and shit…and the economy is all fucked up for the average nigga out here. That nigga needs to get his ass off that chair and come to the hood and walked down Marcy Avenue and see how real niggas be living." Duncan paused for a second to wipe his eyes. "How's a nigga supposed to eat and wipe his ass and there ain't no fucking jobs out here." Duncan waved his arm to the side in frustration as he turned away from Marcus.

"So true, man," Marcus said. "That was a few years ago; so how you making out now otherwise?"

"You know what, man," Duncan said with false confidence. "I'm a new person now. I've been doing some deep meditation and soul searching. I don't need material things to be happy if I am one with the universe. It is all about balance and being able to tune into cosmic energy, you know. I am happy living a simple life with no bills to pay, no landlord to bother me every fucking month. Life is just simple for me right now."

"Where do you live now and how you manage out here?" Marcus interrupted him.

"Listen man, I am trying to survive out here, you know?" Duncan continued by stroking his jaw in a nervous gesture, as sweat poured out from his brow. "Right now I'm staying at a temporary housing complex in Bushwick. They got a soup kitchen in there too, and the food ain't bad if I say so myself."

Marcus looked disappointed and tried to avoid eye contact with Duncan who contradicted himself. "You mean like a homeless shelter? It's all good, I know how it is, it's rough out there like you said…It's a hard knock life living in the hood, trust me, I know."

Marcus remained silent and rubbed his eyes and waited for Duncan to respond. "Actually, I have child support problems of my own. I'm due in court in a few days."

"Oh yeah," said Duncan

"Yeah, man. You know Thelma, right?"

"Yeah, I know who you are talking about."

Marcus began to tell Duncan about the night he slept with Thelma and wish he used a rubber like he did all the other nights.

"She distracted me, that night," said Marcus. "She made sure I didn't wear one that night. She never thought I would end up in jail. I would give her money from the hustling I did throughout the day. It was when I stopped giving her money, was when thing began to change."

"She set your ass up," Duncan whispered.

"The bitch had to find a way to get money out of me; she never thought I would end up in jail, though."

"So now she gonna try to milk you huh?"

"There is no way out of this shit, for real."

"I hope everything goes well for you."

"You too, man," Marcus said extending his hand to Duncan.

"I'm sure we'll run into each other again. Peace."

"Peace."

The two men embraced and Marcus walked off.

Marcus woke up to begin another day of searching for work. While he lay on the couch staring at the ceiling, doubt entered his mind. He allowed it to entertain his thoughts. He wondered if he was wasting his time, going out there day after day putting in applications and not hearing anything from anyone. Every morning, he would wake up with a burning sensation in the middle of his chest. Each day the fire seemed to get stronger as each doubtful thought entered his mind. A feeling of helplessness began to paralyze him from the waist down. It became harder for him to get out of bed each morning. It became a great struggle, indeed. He would rather stay in bed forever, then to face the reality of never being able to find employment. "Supposed I can never get a job," Marcus whispered to himself. An unexpected thought began to creep into his mind which he prayed he would never have to consider. It was the same thought that landed him in jail thirteen years ago.

"Marcus, you ain't never gettin' out of bed, boy," His mother said.

"What's for breakfast?"

"You'll know when you make it."

"All right, Ma, I hear ya," Marcus smirked.

"Are you ready for your court day tomorrow?"

"Oh shit, I almost forgot."

His mother shook her head and walked pass her son lying on the sofa.

"Know how the fuck I'm I going to pay child support?" Marcus mumbled to himself.

Not paying child support meant going back to jail. Going back to jail meant no freedom and being subjected to the penal system. Marcus at once felt the trap that was set for him and many other black males. He knew and read about it intellectually at the prison library, but to feel and experience it on an emotional and psychological level was another thing, in and of itself. For the first time, this instance, it frightened him to his core. For the first time since returning home from prison, he felt there is no way out of his present reality, something he wished he could avoid. The thought that death by suicide might be his only way out, hit him like an arctic wind rushing over a frozen lake. No one would hire him because of his criminal record, no one would loan him money because of his criminal record, and no one would give him a second chance because of his criminal record, let alone his race, which made it even harder.

Marcus, as he sat on the couch, began to see the system as a death cycle and a castration apparatus. The system forced him to question his manhood and didn't allow him to be a man. The system exposed his weaknesses and showed him what he really was, not someone who was economically capable of providing for self, but a perpetual boy with male features.

CHAPTER FOUR

Marcus stood and began to feel nervous about the possible outcome of events that was about to unfold.

"The case before me Thelma Hill v. Marcus Carlton in Kings County Family Court…"

The judge's voice began to fade away from his perception. Marcus wished he could disappear from where he was. He had walked all the way to the court house from his home. He tried to avoid looking at Thelma who was a few arm's length away from him.

"Mr. Carlton."

Marcus quickly came to his senses and looked up at the man behind the desk.

"Mr. Carlton, the State requires that you pay child support," the judge said.

The judge looked at him with distain and malice.

"While you were in prison, Mr. Carlton," the judge continued. "You were unable to make payments; however, the court expects you to pay now that you are out of prison."

The judge, an elderly man in his seventies, moved his glasses down and looked at Marcus over the rim with sharp eyes. "While you were in prison, the plaintiff, made claims against you for payments; those payments are still due, and you are require to make payments as soon as possible." The judge took his glasses off completely and laid them to the side. "Are you currently working?"

"No, your honor," Marcus said nervously.

"Are you currently seeking employment?"

"Yes, your honor. The market is pretty tight right now, but I am still looking."

"Ok, once you have attained employment your wages will be subjected to garnishment, do you understand?"

"I understand, sir."

"Mr. Carlton, if for any reason you are unable to make payments to the plaintiff within the next four to five month from now, you may be subjected to contempt of a court order which can result in imprisonment. I understand that you been in prison for an assault and armed robbery offense and I wouldn't want you to end up spending more time in prison. I would strongly suggest you resolve this current issue."

"Your honor, I will try to do the best I can."

"Your honor, can I say something," Thelma stated abruptly.

"You may."

"A few days ago he, excuse me, Marcus came to my apartment and violated my space, and forced his way into my apartment pushing me out of the way."

"Come on man, I wanted to see my daughter," Marcus interrupted.

"I asked you not to come in," Thelma said turning her head towards Marcus.

"I just got out of jail," Marcus became angry as he proceeded to talk over his ex-girlfriend who began to agitate him. "All you had to do was just let me see Keisha."

"Excuse me," said the judge trying to get their attention.

Marcus and Thelma continued to argue back and forth

like two wild dogs completely unaware of their surroundings.

"Excuse me, for the last time," the judge said raising his voice.

They both stopped talking and turned their faces towards the judge.

"Why did you go to the plaintiff's home?" The judge looked at Marcus with such contempt that he could feel a burning sensation in his gut lit up like the sun.

"I wanted to see my daughter, your honor."

"Did you have permission to go there?"

"I didn't think I needed permission, sir."

"Did the defendant touch you in any way," The judge looked over at Thelma.

"Yes he did…he hit me with his elbow and went straight to my living room where my daughter was…"

"Come on man," Marcus interrupted, raising his arms in frustration. Marcus tried hard to contain his anger, but unfortunately the judge saw him clinched his fist and smacked it against his left hand.

Thelma continued, "After he hit me, he grabbed my daughter, Keisha, I told him to stop and leave, and he wouldn't. I'd do nuttin' to him."

"I see that you had a restraining order against you at one time. In the meantime I'm ordering you not to go near the plaintiff or near her daughter until the Court have heard this matter; is that understood?"

"Your honor, I didn't hurt this woman…"

"Is that understood?" The judge exclaimed.

Not being able to see his daughter made Marcus more upset.

"Yes, your honor."

The court adjourned. Marcus walked out of the court room, frustrated and humiliated from what took place. He had made up his mind, at that moment that the court order wasn't going to prevent him from seeing his daughter. He would find a way, one way or another, to see her.

Marcus was awoken out of bed by a commotion that was heard outside the corridor of his apartment unit. He noticed his mother slowly creeping out of her bedroom door. She also heard the chattering from outside. There was noise also coming from outside the living room window. It was no later than 4:30am in the morning. What the hell could be cooking outside at this time of night, he thought to himself.

It was just before dawn and a cool breeze blow through the window, pushing the curtains so often, in a ghostly manner. As his mother walk towards the apartment door, he quickly peeked out the window, only to see flashing lights. There was a small group of people standing around in their pajamas and robes across the street from where the police cars were.

A crying could be heard from the corridor; it was a neighbor's voice explaining something about someone being shot.

The neighborhood had been a haven for drug users for years, especially since the past four years. People from other communities in Brooklyn would come to Marcy for a quick high. Marcy was officially the crack capital of New York.

"Oh God, I hope it's not my son," the lady grabbed her head while pacing back and forth in her night gown.

"Let me put some clothes on and go down stairs," Marcus told his mother who was consoling the next door neighbor.

As Marcus arrived on the streets, he saw police cars and an ambulance. There was somebody in the ambulance already. There were markings on the floor in the shape of a body where the person was killed. He was able to see one of his friends in the other building around the corner. It seems as if he been out there for a while. He went over to him to see if you knew what took place.

"Yo Mack, was up, man," Marcus said as he approached his friend, who seemed to be disenchanted with the events that had just taken place.

"Nah man, they shot Farod, yo," Mack said removing his headphones from his ears.

"Who?" Marcus replied. "Who is Farod?"

"Where you been? I know you just came out of the pen and shit, but damn homie…"

Marcus tried to recall the name but couldn't.

"He just dropped an album the other day," Mack said sharply as he turned off his Walkman. "I was just listening to it on my new Walkman."

"Oh him," Marcus recalled shaking his head.

"Yeah him, muthafuca, he signed a contract with some niggas in L.A."

"Who shot him?"

"We don't know yet."

"You know, I looked out my window and I saw all them people outside."

"Usually," Mack said turning his head back and forth. "When you see this much crowd of people gathering in a place like this, it means that the person who got killed was not the average nigga that you be seeing walking around here."

Marcus remained silent while absorbing what was going on around him. It was not what he had expected to see when he returned from prison. The crowd slowly began to grow as people knew who the victim was.

Police officers from the NYPD Homicide Unit could be seen walking up and down the streets surveying the area for evidence; some were questioning residents. The police had put up a row of wooden barricades and yellow tape around certain parts of the street where the killing had taken place. A couple of officers in blue uniform had walked by and looked over at Marcus and Mack with a look of suspicion, but kept on walking.

"I've been here for years," Mack continued, "and see niggas get stabbed, beat down, shot, you name it...usually a hand full of niggas comes out and it's back to business as usual...nobody gives a fuck."

"I hear you, man, I just came out to see what was going on," Marcus said. "But, I check you later, I'm out."

Marcus was able to gather more information as sunrise approached. He headed up stairs to his apartment unit. A ghostly image appeared on the neighbor's face as he made the final turn that lead to his apartment.

"Oh my god, who was it?" she said holding her head.

"It was a guy who lived around the corner named Farod. He was an aspiring rapper who was doing pretty well for himself. I heard he have an album out."

"Who could've did some shit like that to him?" his mother asked.

"Some say the police, some say jealous niggas who live here," said Marcus.

"What?" his mother asked.

"Another person told me," Marcus said. "They were looking for some drug dealers that shot at a police car that was patrolling the buildings, a few weeks ago. From what I heard, the cops might have mistaken Farod for the dealers."

His mother sighed, "Seems like no one can ever escape from Marcy. It's like a curse. Why is it always the good ones that always gets killed?"

"I don't know, Ma," Marcus said as he tried to come to grips with the events that just took place.

That night after the incident of the shooting, Marcus met up with a couple of people in the community to discuss the recent events, near the playground on Nostrand Avenue. It was a crowd of community organizers who were angry over the death of the rapper.

Besides being a somewhat popular figure at Marcy, Marcus had come to realized that Farod was also involved in community organizing and youth programs. He became a symbol of hope for many of the youths in the projects. He had dropped out of high school like most youths and started dealing drugs, but then found a passion for music. There were eight people in the crowd at the playground discussing the incident. One lady, who appeared to be very emotional, spoke.

"That shit ain't right, how are we supposed to be safe in our community when the people who are supposed to protect us are killing us?"

"He was just walking home from the studio," said a young man wearing a Yankee T-shirt, who claimed to be a close friend of the rapper. "All of a sudden I heard bang, bang from my living room...l looked out my window and saw him lying on the ground. I know niggas be acting funny when they see you making moves and shit...like you not supposed to better yourself...Sometimes I gotta act like a damn loser just to stay alive in this fucking place, yo...you know, like I ain't doing shit with my life. That's how it is with black folks."

A heavy set man with dread locks, a thick beard and a hint of afrocentricity in his overall demeanor, stood out from the rest. He commanded attention from the group and got it. His voice was somewhat moderate, but defined. Whenever he spoke, he would step back and extend his arms as if he needed room.

"This is just another way of maintain power over us," the bearded man said with anger in his voice. "Stanley was a threat to them…I'm just saying. If you listen to his lyrics, he rap about our struggles, he raps about capitalism and how the system preys on the poor, the weak, and the down-trodden. Don't believe the shit you hear! He was a fucking target, trust me."

Marcus had come to find out from his friend, that the rapper's real name is Stanley Cummings.

"Stanley lived with his mother and two younger brothers, but was planning on moving out after he signed a record deal with some niggas in L.A. Stanley never had a chance. The record deal was minor… it was a stepping stone for him. Rap music was one if not the only outlet for young dudes to escape the cycle of poverty." The bearded man looked down and shook his head as he stroked the hair on his chin.

"So you knew, Farod?" Marcus asked.

"Man, I known this cat since he was going to elementary school." The bearded man raised and dropped his arms in distress, shaking his head. "It ain't like I don't know who I'm dealing with. He was one of those types of dudes that don't bother nobody, you know what I'm saying?"

"Yeah, I feel you," Marcus said nodding his head.

"There is always some shit going on at Marcy. If it ain't one thing it's another," a lady within the crowd said.

The bearded man looked down at the floor and wiped the sweat from his forehead. "I remembered when Wesley got shot because his baby mama told the police he was carrying a gun."

"Wesley, who's that," someone said.

"He's not a rapper," the breaded man said. "But he's a dude that lives here, and he wrote a few lyrics for some other rappers here in New York…just hustling you know."

"When was this?"

"Nigga, where you been?"

"I just came back to Marcy not too long ago," Marcus

replied. "I've been in the joint for a few years."

"Been in the joint?"

"Yeah, man."

"You see, that's the thing, man, it's like we are living inside a box, a prison and the system just forces you to get into trouble," the bearded man said.

"I see what you're saying," Marcus said in a detached way.

"No, you don't, there is no way out!" The man shouted, with frustration.

"So, what about you?" Marcus asked.

"I was born here. I been here since I was a baby, you hear?" The beard man looked around at the others that were left, standing, listening to him preach. "There have been many times that I tried to leave this god forsaken place of a shit hole. Once I tried to become a bus driver, but they told me because I was a felon, I couldn't get behind the wheels. Next, I tried to get a loan to open a bar down the street on Bedford Avenue; they turned me down because I had no credit history and income. I can't get a job because I have a felony record on my fucking back."

"How did you end up going to jail?" Marcus asked.

"I hanged around the wrong crowd when I was a teen…heroin running, you know, I got caught with a bag of it."

"You too didn't have a father growing up, right?"

"Isn't that the case for everybody here?"

"Here's the thing though," Marcus gestured to make a point, "Do you have any children?" Marcus looked at the bearded man.

"Yeah, I have four children."

"…with the same mother?"

"No."

"That's my point," Marcus said smiling. "Your children are being raised without a father just like you did."

"So, what are you sayin'?"

"I'm saying we are living in a cycle," Marcus said. "And getting out of it takes a great deal of effort. Those children of yours will grow up and continue the cycle of fatherless children if they don't change. I read about this in the prison library."

"So you're teaching me now?" the bearded man seems a little annoyed with Marcus. "Shut the fuck up, man."

"No!" Marcus shouted back at him. "Why you so fucking angry all of a sudden?"

"Nigga, you don't know me…homeboy."

Marcus could see that the bearded man was beginning to become combative by his arm gestures and his dead stare. He knew he had to de-escalate the situation fast or the two of them may end up fight before it's all done.

"He wasn't saying anything bad about you," said someone in the group. "He's just trying to make a point, that's all."

"Some of us don't understand that solving the problem starts with us," Marcus said.

"You know you are absolutely right." said the lady with the blue shirt on. "I'm trying to teach my daughter not to go down the same path I took years ago…but it's so hard with all the peer pressure in school and all."

"I know what ya mean," Marcus replied. "I gotta go, see you guys later."

Everyone departed peacefully, and Marcus walked back to his apartment. There were a few police officers stationed outside the buildings. There were some parts that were taped off to prevent contamination of the scene. He managed to get to his apartment and his mother had just finished cooking breakfast. He never complained about the food when in comparison to what he had to endure for thirteen years. He began to reminisce about how he had to pretend, when he was in prison, he was eating Mollie's Fish & Chips on Nostrand

Avenue, it was a way to get the food down his throat and into his stomach. The food he endured for thirteen years was horrible; no seasoning, salt, or taste. The food he was eating now was quite a relief. He realized that a part of him had a problem of giving up the routine of having to eat at a certain time of the day. He was not used to the freedom he was now experiencing; freedom to eat whenever he wanted to and whatever he wanted to. When he was in prison, that responsibility was given to someone else. He never had to cook, buy or steal his next meal, or worry where it was coming from. It was always there at the same time every day. It was a paradox he became aware of, but fought hard to ignore.

CHAPTER FIVE

The idea of having nothing to do troubled him. Marcus wanted to do something. He was bored. He felt he needed to be a contributing member of society. Staying home at his mother's one bedroom apartment was no place for a grown man to be, he thought to himself. He had to find that opportunity that would enable him to start a new life. His allowance from his mother was not enough for him to get started. None of his job applications ever came through for him. Depression began to set in, again. He just about gave up on finding employment. Each passing day began to seem like eternity. A dark feeling of despair gripped him again as he looked through the kitchen window. The world outside had become a dangerous playground; it was unpredictable and misleading. He found himself staying indoors more often than ever. The fear of going back to prison crippled his will to move about. Only his daughter could get his mind off of things.

"I going to go see Keisha," Marcus said to his mother who had just finished eating breakfast.

"You know what happened the last time, boy," his mother

responded.

"Yeah, but this time it's going to be different."

"What do you mean?"

"She goes to school, doesn't she?"

"Yeah, she does," his mother said dragging the words and looking intensely at her son. "Boy, you better not do nothing stupid you know"

"I won't."

"What you goin' do…go to her school?"

"Yeah," Marcus said smiling.

His mother turned around from the stove, wearing a frown on her face. The woman only met her granddaughter twice. She had hoped that she could have helped raise her.

"I would love to see her, Marcus," his mother said teary eyed.

"I could get in deep trouble if I brought her here."

"I know."

"I'm sure she would love to see her grandmother."

"She's the only grandchild I have," his mother said placing her hand over her face, tilting her head downward.

"I got to go."

"Are you going to see her now, or…?"

"No, I'm going to wait when she is going home from school."

Marcus waited across the street from the school. It would only be a couple of minutes until the school emptied out its students for the day. He knew it was risky, but worth it. Getting caught seeing his daughter without supervision was all he needed to end up back where he started. Why would he get in trouble, he taught to himself, after all, he's just going to say 'hello'.

Moments later a herd of young children stormed out of

the metal door, running in different directions. One student wearing an oversize glasses ran passed him, bumped into him and tripped on to the concrete pavement. Luckily the kid was able to brake his fall on the grassy pavement with his book bag. More children came out running, but no sign of Keisha, though. Marcus began to walk pass the fleeing students when he saw a young lady walking with another female student. She had on black jeans and a gray spring jacket. Her braids extended pass the side of her face partly covering her checks. She had a light brown complexion and dark brown eyes that conveyed her innocence. Her delicate frame and her hunch back gait reminded him of her mother when they first met many years ago. Marcus had recognized his daughter.

"Keisha," Marcus said looking at her as he walked towards her. "Is that you?"

The young lady looked up at him, and for a second, recognized who the man was, staring at her. She beckoned for her friend to walk on without her.

"Keisha, are you waiting for your mother?"

"No, I usually take the bus home, but today I have after school dance class."

"So, are you happy to see me?"

"Yeah," she said sheepishly as she adjusted her book bag on her shoulders and pulled back a strand of braids that had moved in front of her eyes.

Marcus' mouth became dry and he could feel his heart pulsating in his neck. He didn't know how to continue the conversation. He did not know how to steer the conversation in such a way that would not harbor any emotional feeling within her. He realized that it was a delicate situation regarding the future of any relationship between him and his daughter.

"I know I haven't been in your life," Marcus managed to say holding his chin. "But I want that to change that. The system has made it hard for us to see each other, you know."

"I have to go to dance class," Keisha said looking at some of the other students who walked passed them.

"I know, but...I want to spend some time with you," Marcus pleaded.

They walked slowly down to the end of the block. Keisha began to feel a little wary about being with a man that she barely knew.

It just occurred to Marcus, how strange for them to be concerned that he may get in trouble for talking to his own daughter. Why should she be concerned with being with him? Shouldn't that be a good thing? It should be something that should actually be encouraged, by the system, was his thought at the moment.

"There is someone that I want you to meet," he said as he turned towards his daughter who barely made eye contact with him.

"Who?" she said.

"Your grandmother; you haven't seen her in a long while, haven't you?"

Keisha made direct eye contact with her father for the first time. His words had struck a clear-sounding bell that seemed to resonate inside her heart.

"I told her that I was going to your school today," he said. "I wanted to bring you back to the house to see her, just for a little while, that's all."

"But what about my class?" she whispered.

"You don't have to go today. Let's catch the bus at the corner," he said looking over at the bus stop.

Keisha was very reluctant, but having the chance to see her grandmother again would be a heartfelt experience.

The two walked to the bus stop. Not many words were exchanged between them. Marcus felt awkward; he wasn't used to seeing his daughter at such an older age. The last time he could remember seeing his daughter was when her mother brought her to the penitentiary to see him. He never had a chance to bond with her growing up, and it was displayed in her behavior; she was acting like he was some fellow she had just met that evening. He felt as if the system had robbed him of being a father to her.

Throughout the bus trip they hardly looked at each other. People on the bus knew they were together, but it didn't give a good impression to see him with a teenager that wasn't his daughter. No one would think, by the way they were acting, that they were father and daughter. No hugs, no smiles, no friendly conversation or exchanges of jokes; it was all emotionless gestures and nods every now and then.

When they arrived at the apartment, he opened the door. There was no one in the living room.

"Have a seat," he said pointing to the sofa.

Keisha sat down on the sofa. She looked around warily, arching her shoulders and folding her lips in an introverted display of humility.

"She's not here," he said coming from his mother's bedroom. "Be careful with that sofa that is also my bed."

They both laughed briefly.

A long silence engulfed the room. It became uncomfortable for the two of them. Nothing was said for a few moments before he broke the silence.

"I know we never really got a chance to talk. I want to say that I am sorry that I was never there for you when you were growing up, Keisha. I know it must've been difficult for you not having a father around and all."

Keisha remained silent and looked straight ahead staring at the front door.

"You see Keisha, while I was in prison all 'dem years, I

met a lot of brothers who became aware of the system and how it affected them and the people in their lives. They wanted to do something about it; so they began reading books in the prison library. You see, I became one of those people…and I'm still learning. One of the things I've read about, was the effect of not having a father around, and how it can have an impact on a child's life, like yourself," Marcus said as he gently touched his daughter on her arm. "This absence creates a void, is what the book called it, which can create serious problems for a child later on in life. Problems like resentment or still searching for the father you never had in the wrong type of men, hoping to fill a void and seeking attention to get it…you know what I mean? I don't want you to end up like that, Keisha."

"I wanted you to be there for me…for my birthdays, but you were never there. I was told you never cared," Keisha interrupted and mumbling her words as she sat at the edge of the sofa with her elbow on her knees and her head tilted down towards the floor.

"Who told you that I never cared," Marcus exclaimed, "Who the fuck told you that?"

"Why you didn't come see me when I was in the hospital?"

"I was in jail, how could I visit you, you know I was locked up!"

Silence prevailed for a few seconds as Marcus tried to reconcile.

"Aren't you happy to see me?"

"I guess," Keisha said shrugging her shoulders.

"What do you mean you guess?"

"I don't know you."

"But I'm your father!"

"I know, but I don't know you," Keisha's voice became

faint as emotions began to set in.

"Well, then act like I'm your father, then," he said as he become irritated that his daughter wasn't showing him the affection he had expected from her.

"What do you want me to do, I have a step-father," Keisha said holding back tears.

"I don't want to hear that," he exclaimed. "That damn mother of yours screwing up your head with all 'dem different niggas coming into the house and shit."

Keisha began to cry. "I don't know what you are talking about, dad," Keisha began wiping her face. "What different men?"

She began to sob, burying her face in her hands. He sat on the edge of the sofa and patted her shoulder gently.

"I'm sorry, sweetie, I'm sorry," Marcus said as he moved closer to her on the couch.

Marcus began consoling her with one arm draped around her frail shoulders. This was the first time he held his daughter since she was a child. As he placed his hand on her shoulders, he said, "I want to be there for you. I love you, Keisha." He knew she was feeling abandoned and he wanted to correct the wrongs that were done in his absence.

"I love you too," she mumbled.

Marcus was surprise at the last statement she made. It was unexpected and haunting, but yet a relief.

"Listen, Keisha," he said clearing his throat. "I am sorry I wasn't there for you when you were growing up. I know how it is for a young girl to not have a father in her life. It's the same thing that happened to your mother and my mother, and it ain't going to happen to you. I want to end this cycle with you. I want to be there for you, now and forever."

She lifted her head up from her lap and wiped away her tears and spoke. "Graduation came and I wanted you to be there but you weren't. When I was young there was no one to take me to the playground because mom was too afraid of the boys that be on the street corners acting stupid. There was a rat in the apartment that frightened me for three days because mom was too afraid to get it out…the Super kept saying he would come but never came. Then there was Father's Day and mom just told me to shut up about it and forget it…"

Their conversation was interrupted by someone opening the front door to the apartment.

"Grandma!" Keisha exclaimed as she jumped up and ran to the woman holding a large paper bag in her arms. The woman quickly placed her groceries on the floor and grabbed her granddaughter tightly causing the two to almost trip over the bag of groceries.

"How's my baby doing," the elderly woman looked her granddaughter over from head to toe. "You've grown so big, you almost a woman now. Daddy brought you here to see me? Bless his heart."

"Ma, she can't stay here too long, remember?" Marcus got up from the sofa and walked over to the two women as they embrace each other.

"I know, I know, you can stay for dinner, no?"

"I have to get home soon. My mother is waiting for me; I don't want her to ask me where I've been," Keisha said looking concerned.

"I don't want you to get in trouble, but I'm so happy to see you, it's been a while hasn't it?" the elderly woman was filled with grief as she wished her granddaughter good bye. "You need Marcus to walk you home, sweetie?"

"No, grandma, I'll be safe."

"Let me walk you downstairs, Keisha," Marcus said.

After the two walked down the stairs and through the doors, Marcus grabbed his daughter by the shoulders and said,

"Keisha, I know I haven't been a good father, there was nothing I could have done, things happen in life. That was the card I was dealt, and I had to work with the hand that was given to me. Now that I am here, I will work to make sure that you grow up to be the best woman you can be. When you become eighteen, we won't have to hide anymore. If you ever need anything let me know. Call the house, if you ever need anything, you hear? I'll see you again soon. Oh and by the way, I still care about your mother. I know she is bitter about my circumstances and all, but I'll do what I have to do to win her back, you hear?"

"I understand," Keisha said waving her hand as she walked away from his presence. "Good bye, daddy."

Marcus watched his daughter as she walked down Flushing Avenue. He felt there was a growing connection between the two of them. However, he felt her mother had turned her against him based on unwanted circumstances that took place in his life.

He went back upstairs to his apartment with feelings of hope in his eyes.

His mother approached him as he entered the living room.

"Thanks for bring Keisha here," his mother said.

"No problem," he said.

His mother turned around and pointed to the table in the living room.

"There's a letter on the table," she said.

Marcus opened the letter. "Ah, fuck man," he said as he read and threw the letter to the ground. "I can't believe this, again, yo what the fuck!"

"Marcus, please not in the house."

"I ain't got no money, yo."

"What is it, she looking for child support money?"

"She knows I ain't working, but she is still hounding me like a bitch."

"You know if you don't pay, it will add up."

"And then I will never pay it off. I already owe money from when I was in jail. Plus she has some nigga supporting her and she's still fucking with me. What they want me to do, steal it?" Marcus paced the kitchen searching for answers. "I aint going."

"What you mean you ain't going," his mother said.

"They can't force me to go."

"But, you know what will happen to you…that's a summons you know!"

"I know what it is Ma, I know what it is."

"Please don't start acting like your father."

"Ma, don't go there," Marcus replied, looking at his mother sternly. "I never met the man."

"You did, you were just too young to remember."

"I know you told me the story many times before."

"It's just that he turn is back on responsibilities; I don't want you to end up like him."

"I know, you told me that many times before."

"And I gon' tell you many times again, ya hear?"

"Ok, so you made bad choices like I did," Marcus stated.

"I didn't know he was going to turn out like he did," his mother screamed walking toward him. "Stop trying to get smart with me boy, I'm a grown woman and I'm your mother, ya hear!"

"I know, I'm just saying."

"You ain't saying shit!" his mother swings her arm towards him and almost hit him in the face.

Marcus quickly moved back to prevent her hand from hitting him in the face. "Ma, why do you have to get so emotional?"

"I ain't getting emotional; I'm just about to talk some sense into ya head, that's all."

"Every time he comes up in a conversation, you get emotional."

His mother stopped and collected her thoughts for a second. She looked towards the ceiling and spoke.

"I loved your father...I really did. It just that...oh, I don't want to talk about it you know," his mother sat down on the chair at the kitchen table. She placed her head down and began to cry. "You know, he was the only man I ever cared about, but he gone hang around the wrong company, just like your brother did. I tried, I tried to warn him but he wouldn't listen to me that day, he just won't. You know a day never goes by that I don't think about him or that brother of yours. You might have been too young to remember that day, but I do, every day. Every time you leave this house, I worry. I know how it is out there. This world is like a jungle. You never know what could happen...who or what you may end up losing at any given time."

Marcus walked up to the women crying with her head on the table, cushioned by her forearm. "Look Ma, I got to go."

The thought of seeing his mother like that, in that state, reminded him of his daughter and why she must be a part of his life. It hurt him to remain there in her presence, seeing her in her present condition. He couldn't help her at that point.

"I don't want you to go outside, today," his mother added.

"Why?" Marcus exclaimed.

"I just think you should stay home more often, that's all."

"I haven't been outside since I woke up."

"Go if you have to."

"I'll be safe, Ma."

Marcus showed up for his court date. It was his second appearance in two months. The judge appeared on the bench. He was the same judge from his last appearance. The black cladded man looked at his binder. There was a conversation between the judge and his baby mama, but his daydreaming clouded his hearing. He was so concern about making money he could barely hear the judge's voice calling him.

"Mr. Carlton...Mr. Carlton!" The judge shouted.

"Sir, I'm sorry, my mind was somewhere else."

"I suggest you pay attention."

"I will," Marcus could hear his heart racing as he tries to come to grips with what was happening before the judge acknowledged him.

"I was asking you, why haven't you been making payments, to the plaintiff?"

"Your honor, I haven't been able to find a job."

The judge left his seat, and walked back to his chamber. His actions seem quite habitual. Moments later the elderly man returned to his bench.

"Here's the deal, I understand you're having trouble securing employment, however that doesn't excuse you from paying child support. From now on, I order you to keep track of all the attempts you make on finding work. I want you to keep a record, in other words, of all the places and name of all the employers, with the addresses, phone numbers and everything, of all the companies that you apply, for employment. On your next court hearing I want you to present it to the Court as evidence of your effort to find work; is that clear?"

"Yes, your honor."

"And for any reason, the Court believes that your effort is unsatisfactory, I will order you to do jail time. This is not a joke! I expect you to find work in ninety days from tomorrow, is that clear?"

"Yes."

"By the way, the Court expects to see at least five potential employers per day, on that list."

Marcus sighed and nodded his head.

"Court adjourned."

"There won't be a next time; I am not going to look for work. It's a waste of time," Marcus whispered to himself as he left the court room.

CHAPTER SIX

The next morning, on his way to the barber shop, Marcus recalled the rejections he experienced at the places he visited on his quest for employment. He remembered the Korean owner at the dry cleaners, who took forever to see him, and then took his application and never looked directly at him or offers him a handshake. Then there was the Dominican manager at the local grocery store who said he only hires family members. Marcus began to feel like he was trapped in a box. He considered writing lyrics and become an aspiring rapper, or at least a backup rap singer. It required a lot of creativity on his part, something he was not used to doing. Getting into the industry would be a major task in and of itself. He didn't know of anyone to ask for help. If there was any place to find answers, it was the barber shop.

The barber shop seemed quite empty on a Saturday afternoon; nevertheless, his barber, Carter, was working that day. Carter was sitting on the barber's chair. He noticed someone sitting on the sofa talking to him. He didn't know who the other guy was, but he knew he'd seen him before. He was a conspicuously short and muscular character who wore his baseball cap backwards. He also had a brown leather jacket which had a patch on the left side that displayed a picture of the continent of Africa. There were other symbols, on his jacket, such as a square and a compass with the letter G. He had an aura that expressed confidence and perseverance. It was more than just the way he leaned over with his elbows on his knees, while sitting on the couch, it was a certain discipline he portrayed.

When Marcus entered the barber shop the two men were sitting across from each other, but separated from everyone else as if, having a private conversation. Carter noticed him when he walked in. Carter immediately stood up and adjusted his pants that were slouching below his waist.

"Yo wad up, man," Carter said while holding his hand above his shoulder to shake hands with Marcus who quickly turned around and looked at the man who Carter was talking to.

"I've been good, you know," Marcus said.

"Have a seat," Carter gestured.

"The usual," Marcus said walking over to the chair and sitting down.

Marcus looked at the man, who Carter was talking to and knotted his head.

"How's it going," said the man in a dark blue baseball cap.

"Yo, you remember Derek back in High School?" Carter asked.

"Yeah, yeah, now I remember, oh all right, yeah," Marcus gleamed at Derek's face recalled seeing him at the basketball court. "You played ball with Marc and them back in school?"

"You still remember that shit," Derek said smiling.

"Whatever happened to Marc?"

"I don't know, man, I heard he's in jail."

"Damn!"

A few minutes passed and Carter was just about finishing Marcus' haircut.

"So, how is everything going with you up there at Marcy?" Carter asked Marcus as he finished shaping up the back of Marcus' neck.

"I don't know how to say this, but, man, my ass is broke."

Carter and Derek began to laugh.

"Man, I have child support payments I got to make, I'm not working, I need new clothes, and I need to see a dentist," Marcus said. "I'd do anything to get out of my situation right now. I've sent out application after application and nothing...no response from nobody."

"You live with your mom's right?" Derek asked, showing concern, stroking his chin and glaring at Marcus.

"I live with my mother; they moved her into to this small ass apartment when I was in the joint. I actually sleep on the sofa, it's that bad," Marcus chuckled as he beckoned to remind Carter to shave down his mustache.

"You ain't looking for work, nigga?" Carter said as he reached for his other electric razor. He waited for Marcus to reply before proceeding.

"I just told you, I looked everywhere. It's the same old bullshit stories."

"And you got a felony too, right?" Carter said.

"Yeah, that just make it worst for me, you know. With a felon, you get no second chance, especially if you're black."

"I know how you feel," Carter said. "I really do."

"I can't sleep on that damn sofa anymore; it's hurting my back an' shit."

Derek stroked his chin as if in deep contemplation, and then asked, "What you plan on doing?" Derek stood up straight and then leaned back against the pillow behind him. "What I mean is...eventually you have to do something, right?

Do you plan on living with you mother for the rest of your life?"

"I don't know, I would like to start a business, like go into hip hop or something, you know. I heard in prison that rap music is growing fast," Marcus turned to Derek who was gazing at him. "There's a lot of young cats out there who got talent and who's looking for an opportunity to start something; you know, a way out of the ghetto." Marcus allowed his mustache to be shaped up before continuing. "I hear hip hop is big business these days, especially on the west coast. I may want to look into that, you know. It's hard to get your feet wet, though."

"I'm feeling you, dog," Derek said sharply nodding his head slowly.

"I don't want to go back to jail for not paying no damn child support," Marcus stated.

"I think you'll be just fine," Carter said after spraying alcohol throughout Marcus' head while laughing at his last remark. "We're all set." Carter removed the cloth from around Marcus' neck and look keenly at Derek who looked back at him.

"Thanks," Marcus handed Carter $12.00. "Take care, man."

As Marcus began to walk out the door, Derek walked up to him and said, "Yo, my man, let me ask you something. You say you need money right?"

"Yeah, what's up?" Marcus slowly turned towards Derek.

"Let's go outside and talk for a minute," Derek said as he walked towards the door beckoning Marcus to follow him.

"Hold up, wait for me," Carter said to the other two who were walking out the door. "Yo Doc, I'm leaving for the day," Carter said to the owner of the barber shop who was attending to a client.

Marcus and Derek were already outside waiting when Carter exist the shop. The three men walked down Marcus Garvey Blvd.

"So, how bad you want to make money?" Derek said looking directly at Marcus who seemed a little confused about the question. Marcus wondered why someone who he hardly knew was so concerned about his financial wellbeing. Marcus remained silent, but was slightly nervous, but he managed to move his legs forward.

"Nigga, do you want to make money are not!" Derek exclaimed, "I'm just asking a question. What you worried about?"

"I ain't worried my nigga," Marcus said to him nervously, "You got a job for me or something?"

Derek carefully looked at Carter who had his hands in his pocket and his eyes looking towards the ground.

"Maybe," Derek replied. "Let's cross the street here and walk down that block."

The three walked a few blocks towards Williamsburg, and stopped in front of a check cashing store that was crowded with local customers waiting to cash checks.

"We don't have to stop right in front of the damn place," Carter said with a nervous laughter.

"What you want me to do cash checks for you or something?" Marcus asked looking at the store in front of him. "How much does the job pay?"

The other two men laughed briefly.

"Not quite," Derek said. "Let's walk to the end of the block."

As the three walked down the street to the end of the block, Derek continued, "Every day, six times a week that place cash hundreds of dollars of checks from hard working people who live in this community. In order, for them to cash them many checks a day, they must have a few, better yet I would say at least 50,000 dollars on hand to start out with before they have to replenish."

"Ok, Derek, so what?" Marcus said wetting his lips and baffled.

"What I'm saying is if you want money, you have to go where the money is," Derek said as he noticed Marcus' hands shaking slightly.

Marcus looked at Carter for a moment to get his impression. The two men had discussed the matter before discussing it with Marcus, but had found the right opportunity to bring in another partner.

Marcus could not believe what he was hearing. For a moment he had a sense of uncertainty, yet had a sense of relief. For a few seconds he could feel his blood rushing through his veins. For that moment, it seemed like everything around him had stopped moving. He didn't notice the group of teenage boys on bicycles riding pass him; one of them came too close and almost hit him.

"Yo, watch out," Carter quickly tried to pull Marcus out of the way before the boy on the gray dirt bike almost clipped him on his right arm.

"You all right," Derek asked. "I thought you fell asleep or something."

"Nah, I'm good," Marcus replied.

"Alright then, wake the fuck up then," Derek said. "Are you paying attention?"

"So, what are you saying?" Marcus asked, gazing at Derek.

"I'm saying we need to take what's ours that is all."

"You mean like rob the place?" Marcus whispered.

"Do I gotta spell it out for ya?" Derek whispered back. "What the fuck you think."

Marcus sighed and covered his open mouth with his hand

as it slid down his chin and over his neck. He was in total conflict for a split moment in time. He was plunged deep into a feeling of despair and then to hope and only to fall back into despair again. It was as if life was repeating itself. It was the same scenario that had landed him in prison in the first place.

"So you down or what?" Derek asked sharply.

A grim silence followed, and then Marcus spoke nervously.

"Look man, I just got out of jail not too long ago, I'm trying to change my life around you know, I got a daughter to look after and all; I can't go down that road again. Yes, I can use the money, God knows, but I don't know. Look man, we can start a business together if you want, you know. There are a lot of things we can do, just look around. I don't think this is a good idea. Think about what would happen if we got caught."

"All right, we can start a business, but where we going to get the fucking money from, you got capital?" Derek interrupted him angrily. "That's why we are doing this. Every day I hear the same shit, do this do that', 'do something with yourself'. How the fuck can I start when there is nothing for a nigga to start with."

"Look man …," Marcus exclaimed as he looked down and shook his head.

"No you look!" Derek exclaimed. "Let me ask you something; how the fuck you think them fucking Koreans started that bank in their neighborhood? They come in our hood, start up a business like this one, while a brotha can't start no business because he can't get no loan because he has no capital because he got a criminal record, and then them damn Koreans take our hard earn money, go back into their own community and open up a fucking bank! Where's the justice?"

Marcus was a little surprised and wondered why the other

two would even conceive of risking their lives and freedom for such an undertaken. He felt trapped, like he was put on the spot.

"Look at how they treat our people," Derek said. "They show no respect for us when we patronize their business; no smiles, can't wait for you to leave, an' shit. Remember, we're not stealing their money...we're actually stealing our money back from them."

"I understand what you're saying and all, but I don't know right now, let me think about it, that's all I ask."

"Cool, it's all good, think about then," Derek said. "By the way, I noticed you mentioned something about you wanted to get into the hip hop business."

"Yeah," Marcus said looking surprised.

"I was thinking about starting my own record label. With the money we would get from this fucking place, it would be possible. I would make you and Carter partners if you choose to do this. But do you know how difficult it is to start a label?" Derek asked. "You need a few thousands just to rent a small spot for a studio, and that doesn't include the equipment and legal fees."

Marcus nodded his head and looked away at the cars driving by. For a minute he wanted to disappear.

"Yo, Marcus, we'll talk later," said Carter who shook hands with Marcus before he and Derek left Marcus standing at the street corner.

It's been a week since Marcus last met with Carter and Derek. He tried hard not to contemplate the idea of doing something as stupid as what they proposed. He was beyond that, a new man, not like his father, but a man who could create opportunities for himself, and not have to resort to criminal activities to accomplish what many African Americans have done centuries before him; besides, what's the point of risking freedom for a few bucks, anyway, he thought. Derek wanted him to steal from someone who stole from us. He fell asleep with the idea every day since they last met. There was a part of him that wanted to do it for the money; yet he would risk it all. What bothered Marcus was the fact that he continued day after day, entertaining the idea of taking money from someone, even though he did it before. He was reformed, the system reformed him. He was corrected! He would try not to think about it any longer. However, the idea kept him tossing and turning in bed. His mother began to notice a change in his behavior.

One time during dinner she asked, "Is something bothering you, son?"

"No, mom," he said.

"Well, it sure seems that way, like you have a lot on your mind."

"Money problems, I guess."

"Well I know it hard to get back on ya feet after leaving that jail house, but God will provide and make a way; watch and see."

"I have a lot of decisions to make."

"He will make the right decisions for you."

"It's just that…sometimes I feel like I'm in a box, or a cage for that matter, that's all."

"Marcus, sometimes you just have to take what's yours."

"Even if it's not yours?"

"What the hell do you mean by that?"

"Well, I mean, it's yours, but someone took it from you in the first place."

"Then take it back, if it's yours."

"Thanks, Ma, I knew you would understand."

CHAPTER SEVEN

Marcus woke up the next morning to receive a phone call from Carter who wanted to meet with him that evening. He wanted to meet at the barber shop. He agreed, but later changed his mind after his conscience got the best him. Marcus couldn't believe he was still entertaining the thought of robbing a business and risk going back to jail. He didn't show up for the meeting, nor did he ever call Carter to cancel. He wished the ordeal would go away. It even appeared in his dream the other day.

Marcus woke up one night before the crack of dawn, with cold sweats rolling down his chest. He fought hard to fall back to sleep, but the vision of him eating food from a can, or sleeping in a single 8x15 foot cell with security guards checking his personal belonging twice a day hindered his thought of possibly walking away with huge amounts of cash in his pocket. He stared into the dark living room and waited for the sun to rise. A feeling of nostalgia embraced him. He could almost smell the faint odor of the dirty laundry coming from the corridor. The depression of loneliness gripped him for a moment. "My daughter," he thought. "She needs me, I can't do it." A cool wind blew through the living room window as he gazed through the darkness that engulfed him both physically and mentally.

Marcus walked over to the window, which overlooked the Brooklyn ghetto, of the living room from which he slept. It was the middle of the night and he could not sleep at all.

"Doesn't anyone sleeps in this god forsaken place," he whispered to himself.

Marcus observed the quiet commotions taking place on the street corners outside his apartment. He observed grown men pacing back and forth like ants, some wearing hoodies; others wearing baggie pants below the waist, and long sleeve T-shirts. There seem to be no ultimate aim to what they were doing; groups of men who live their lives to merely survive day to day. They could never see a bigger picture to things or a purpose to life in general, just instant gratification. There was no planning involved in their lives, no goals or aspiration. It was a total waste of existence.

The scenery began to look like a zoo to Marcus who bowed his head before raising his head to look again. That very thought frightened him. The difference between them and him was that he was becoming conscious of his situation. He saw what others couldn't see. There was no evolution taking place whatsoever in front of him. Things were the same way they were ten, twenty, thirty years ago; nothing has changed. The frightening reality is that things most likely will never change.

Marcus noticed a woman who seemed under nourished, as he looked out the window, walked over to one of the men who were smoking a cigarette at the corner. Her hair was unkempt; she had a distorted gait that seemed as if she was walking on ice. The spandex she was wearing was too loose for her thin frame. She started to argue briefly, with the man in front of her. Marcus could barely hear the conversation between them. Afterwards, she reluctantly handed him a bill and they ended the exchange with the man handing her something in a tiny plastic bag.

A few minutes later, a car double parked next to the entrance to the apartment building. A young man in his early twenties walked over to the dark gray car while adjusting his pants, which was falling off his waist. By the time he got to the car, a man wearing a leather jacket with a stern gesture got out of the front passenger side of the vehicle and grabbed the young man by the neck and exchange words with him which Marcus could not hear. The man shoved the young man against the hood of the car.

"How many times nigga, I gotta tell you to keep yo eyes open you dumb motherfucka," the man yelled clenching his fist.

Marcus suddenly recalled that police had raided one of the apartments the other night in his building.

Minutes later the man in the black leather jacket punched the young man in the face. As he fell to the ground, the man kicked him in the stomach repeatedly, causing him to cry in pain. The man began throwing a series of punches and kicks to his face and shoulders. Blood could be seen coming from the young man's face as he lay on the ground trying to protect his face with his forearm. The man then grabbed his leg and dragged him across the concrete floor as a trail of blood could be seen stretching across the front entrance. A scream could be heard from someone saying, "Stop! Leave him alone." The man stopped only to pull out a gun and spoke to the young man lying on the cement floor, who began pleading with him for his life. A small crowd quietly gathered. Some of the people in the area, pretended to be preoccupied with their own business but instead were walking closer to get a better view as they could taste what was about to come to past.

Marcus couldn't take no more of it and began crying; he

wanted to believe what he was seeing was a dream. "I've seen this fucking cycle every day, day in and day out with no end in sight," he said as he slowly drifted away from the window wiping tears from his eyes. "The funny thing is, I would wake up in the middle of the night on another day and see the exact scene play out, like a bad movie every fucking day." Marcus went back on the sofa and rested his head on the pillow. As he looked towards the ceiling, he heard two gun shots, followed, seconds later, by the sound of car tires screeching against the street pavement.

While covering his face with the blanket, he heard the sounds of police sirens moving closer and closer to the building. He could see through the blanket, flashing lights piercing the darkness in his room.

That morning, his mother had told him that the young man who died last night was the second person to be killed from the building in less than a week. The other person, a sixteen year old girl, was shot by police when they raided an apartment on the second floor three days ago. People in the building say that she was shot when she tried to prevent the police from entering the bedroom door. Her brother, however, was arrested along with two other men who were in the apartment at the time. His mother also mentioned that on the news the reporter said that the police had also found several pounds of crack cocaine, two scales, a hand gun, and about twelve thousand dollars' worth of cash stashed behind a radiator.

Marcus' next court meeting was approaching, and he was a bit concerned. He had something figured out. He would tell the Judge that he was going to be a part of his uncle's business. This lie would give him enough time to figure out what he intends to do with his life and how to make money. He didn't want to go back to jail, especially for not paying child support. He did have an uncle in Jamaica, Queens who owned a mechanic shop with his childhood friend. If anything, he would ask him to appear in court in a couple of weeks, on his behalf. His mother had one time asked her brother if he could provide a helping hand, but business was not doing too well, since a small fire destroyed part of the building. The business was merely breaking even ever since.

Today would be the day he would visit his daughter's school again. Marcus wished he could buy something for her. A gold bracelet, a key chain, a watch, ear rings, something she could hold on to, to remember him. He was broke and beaten. The only income he received was from his mother's weekly allowance. He disliked having to ask his mother for money when he was capable and had two hands. He also hated having his daughter see him in such a needy state. He was not a role model for the type of man he want his daughter to aspire to have one day.

Marcus waited near the same spot he waited the last time. A young lady wearing tight blue jeans, with a white sweater, and a new pair of red Jordans approached him. Her hair was braided, and for the first time he'd seen her wearing ear rings. She didn't have that innocence she once had, at least the last time they met. There was a different glow about her, and a radiance engulfed her face made her look older.

"Hi dad," said Keisha. "I didn't know you were coming to see me."

"It's not like I can call you and tell you that I'm coming," Marcus laughed. "Can't I get a hug?"

The two embraced for a few seconds.

"Keisha, how you doing?"

"I'm ok."

"How's your mother doing?"

"She's home."

"What's with the Jordans?"

Keisha didn't answer.

"So, who bought them for you?" Marcus asked, "Or better yet, who gave mommy the money to buy the sneakers for you?"

"Her friend," she said annoyed.

"What friend?" Marcus asked.

"Can we go to the store?" Keisha asked.

"We can go to the store after you tell me who bought those sneakers," Marcus raised his voice.

"Mom's boyfriend," Keisha said as she turned her face away from her father.

"So what else he bought you!"

"I don't know, dad."

"What you mean you don't know," Marcus said trying to get his daughter to look him in the face. "Losing your memory or something."

Keisha didn't want to talk anymore. Marcus was aware of her frustration, but nevertheless, he wanted to get to the bottom of what was happening between his daughter and the man who her mother was dating. The tension between the two grew. The last thing Marcus wanted was to make his relationship with his daughter more unstable.

"Come on man, what that nigga be giving you," Marcus asked.

"Money for school, things like that," Keisha said adjusting her book bag.

"Money, huh," Marcus stated as he nodded his head. "So, he got money and I don't."

"He just help me out on little things, dad," Keisha looked at her father and said, "Please don't get mad."

"Who's mad?"

"I'm just saying."

"Who the fuck is mad," Marcus asked sternly. "He takes you places too?"

"Like, where?" Keisha asked.

"Keisha!" Marcus exclaimed.

"He took us to the movies last week. He wants us to go to Miami to visit his brother, but mom won't go."

Marcus placed his hands in his pants pocket.

"Dad," Keisha said. "I have to get home; I have a project for biology class I have to finish up."

"Answer my question," Marcus said. "Does he take you places with just the two of you?"

"Codie's."

"What's that?"

"They sell burgers and stuff, he owns the place too."

"Why didn't your mother go along?"

"She was getting her hair done."

"After you guys eat the burger and fries, you both went back home?"

"Yeah," Keisha said turning away from her father.

"Does he sleep over sometimes?"

"Yeah, on weekends," Keisha said with an attitude that said, stop asking me questions. "Dad, can I go?"

"Why, what's the rush?"

"My project, I told you."

"Yeah, go finish your fucking project."

Keisha left without saying a word. It was probably the first time Marcus felt like killing himself. Another man providing for his daughter was worse than jail itself. A sense of hopelessness overshadowed him. For a brief moment, he looked into the abyss and saw nothing.

Marcus took Marcus Garvey Blvd home. It began to rain,

and he had no umbrella to shield him from the rain. He pulled his jacket over his head and walked, and occasionally ran when he crossed the streets. He occasionally looked back behind him to see if a gypsy cab was coming up the street. As he jogged to the corner of Myrtle Avenue he could see a familiar face up ahead.

"Yo, Marcus!"

It was Carter. Carter began to wave his arm as Marcus walked toward him. He had just come out of the corner deli with a plastic bag in his hand.

"Come out of the rain, man," Carter quickly moved out from the sidewalk and moved closer to the corner store.

"I hardly recognized you," Marcus lied. "How's it going?"

"Everything's cool, you know," Carter said. "I've been trying to get in touch with you."

"I've been busy, you know, trying to find work and all."

"Yeah, I understand."

"Look man, I don't want to get wet, I got get to get on home, dinner is going to get cold," Marcus laughed as he put his jacket back over his head.

"Hold up, man…listen. Derek wants to talk to you. I know how you feel; but let him speak to you. He's been trying to reach out to you."

"I don't know, man. You guys can do your thing; you know what I'm saying."

"Marcus, you don't have to do anything, dude; just hear what he has to say, that's all."

Marcus nodded his head as he stepped backward into the rain.

"I'm going to give him your number and have him call you, aight?"

"Sounds good, talk to you later," Marcus waved and ran down the street.

When Marcus arrived at the housing units, the usual characters were out and about, loitering on the sidewalk. He witness cars pulling in and out of the projects to greet the young men waiting at the curb. Most times the young men would wait at the bodega too, at the corner smoking weed or drinking forty ounces. Some also waited near the phone booths at the corner of each street, waiting for the phone to ring.

Marcus avoided trouble by keeping his head down and minding his own business. Marcy was no joke, for the most part. Many of the young men carried gun in their waist, and wouldn't hesitate to use it on someone who threatened their source of revenue. Then there were the ones that were easily distinguishable by their particular gait. They were the users or abusers. They were zombie-like; they walked around the projects in a comatose state.

Marcus noticed something disturbing about them when he went to asked one of them where the superintendent's office was moved to, one particular day. Marcus noticed that this one man, in his early fifties with a slim frame, was never able to focus when he looked Marcus in the eyes. It was as if he was looking through h
im into outer space in the distant galaxy. It seemed as if, at least, half the population at Marcy had become soul-less creatures existing solely for the purpose of appeasing their appetite and enriching the underworld that existed there since the outbreak of crack cocaine in 1985.

Marcus was soaked when he got in his apartment. He made it just in time for dinner. The food was still warm on the stove. His mother had already settled in, in her room. After taking a shower, he headed straight to bed.

CHAPTER EIGHT

"Marcus, Marcus!"

Marcus woke to the voice of his mother calling him. It took a while before he realized that he was no longer dreaming. The situation reminded him of the days when the prison guards would do roll calls; and he would jump out of bed for fear of being punished for indolence. This time he was able to catch himself by the time reality kicked in.

"Marcus, boy," the voice screamed.

Wiping the cold from his eyes, Marcus looked up at the figure standing in front of him.

"What, Ma?"

"Don't you hear the phone ring?"

"No."

"All you do is sleep all damn day," his mother said, grabbing her pocket book off the table in the kitchen. "There's a man on the phone, asking for you."

Marcus strolled over to the kitchen table where the phone was laying down of the hook. He couldn't believe that it was after 9:00 o'clock already.

"Marcus, I'm a be away for a few hours, gotta go to the social security office this morning you hear?"

He walked over to the phone and pick it up.

"Hello, who's this?" Marcus asked, clearing his throat and still recovering from a bad dream.

"Yo, nigga," the voice said. "What's up?"

"Who this?"

"Derek."

"Oh, hey…"

"Carter gave me your number; we need to talk."

"Talk about what?"

"Our future."

"It's nice to know I have one."

"Don't be funny, this is serious."

"Look, man I don't know if I can do this, you know?" Marcus stated while pulling a chair from under the kitchen table.

"No, I don't know. I just want to meet with you; and let's talk, that's all."

"Aight, I can do that much," Marcus wiped his dry face with his hand. "That much I can only do for now."

"Let's do this. Meet me tonight …do you know how to get to the Williamsburg Bridge?"

"Yeah, I think so."

"Meet me there."

"Cool. What time?"

"7:30, don't worry, you'll see me when you get there."

"Is Carter coming?"

"Maybe."

"All right, bye."

Marcus contemplated whether he should actually go. He could just not show up and try to avoid seeing either Carter or Derek for the next couple of months. Avoiding them would be hard. Then again, the worst that could happen is that they'll just find someone else. Besides, why they need me, he thought to himself, two people could pull off the job. Marcus began to consider what he would tell Derek if he decides to meet him later on in the day. He began rehearsing what to say to him. He would have to come up with a good excuse. Risking everything is just not worth it. He didn't like the idea of taking something that didn't belong to him. He couldn't image what he would do if someone took something of his.

It was already pass sunset, when Marcus arrived at the entrance to the pedestrian walkway of the Williamsburg Bridge. The air was cool and crisp, with an occasional breeze coming from the East River. There were a few last minute joggers, cyclist, and men with brief cases traveling pass Marcus while the darkness was setting in. There was a lone figure up ahead leaning forward against the fence, wearing a dark gray sweater, blue jeans and construction boots, smoking a cigarette. It was Derek, and he was gazing toward the Manhattan skyline like a voyageur looking to his destination before sail.

"What a view, huh," Marcus said as he came close enough to smell the tobacco blowing in the wind.

"Thought you weren't coming," Derek said with smoking oozing out of his nostrils.

"Nah, man, I'm a man of my word," said Marcus. "Where's Carter?"

"He couldn't make it."

"So, what are you dreaming about, I saw you gazing at the tall buildings?"

"Nigga, I'm tired of dreaming," Derek said turning to look at Marcus for the first time. "There are only two types of people in this world, dreamers and doers; and I'm tired of being a dreamer. That's why I brought you here. I need a partner."

"Yeah, but there are other ways to make money without…"

"Let me ask you something," Derek interrupted. "You ever heard of the robber barons in High School?"

"Yeah, the Carnegies, the Rockefellers, what about 'em.?" Marcus stated looking puzzled.

"That's how they made their money, by robbing the people who worked for them. The difference between them and you is that you got caught the first time. They never got caught; and the money that they made, they were able to build an empire. That's what we got to do! And from now on, we Rockefellers."

A letter J train heading towards Manhattan roared through, interrupting Derek's lecture, but Marcus became intrigued by what he was hearing and continued to listen while enjoying the view.

There was a long pause and Derek covered his eyes momentarily with his right hand and spoke dramatically.

"Every day of my life I searched for opportunities to become the man my folks wanted me to be, but every road I took there were obstacles of racism, unemployment, and peer pressure, you know what I'm saying. All I wanted was an opportunity, a fair and equal chance at life. I was sent to jail because I was carrying weed for somebody. That day police saw me walking down the street, rush me, and frisk me for no fucking reason. They found a bag of weed I was carrying and I got two years in prison for that shit; couldn't get a dissent job after that. I ended up having to drop out of college. I only did a year and a half, too. I went broke and eventually ended up having to live with my grandma's in the fucking projects. The system isn't fair. There has to be a balance; and it is up to us to make that balance."

"Making it balance, by what we are doing?" Marcus interjected.

"What I'm saying is," Derek quickly continued. "You

have to understanding that the strong preys over the weak, and I am tired of being the weak; when I say weak I mean the poor. Nobody gives you shit, you got to take it, you know what I'm saying? You and I can live like kings, just like the people who built this city we looking at; but all we looking for right now is a down payment to get started, that's all…just a down payment to get this record label going."

Derek took his last puff of the cigarette and throws it over the side of the bridge. He felt a sense of relief and smiled because he knew he had aroused the interest of his friend. "You know what I notice, Marcus," Derek said facing his friend. "When I worked at my last job, everybody couldn't wait 'tll Friday, that's right, the weekend. That was the one thing on their fucking minds all day all week, when is Friday going to get here. You could see it in their eyes, every fucking minute, like fucking slaves. But for us, we won't have to look forward to Fridays; everyday will be a Friday for us. You see, the goal is never having to work again; the goal is to have other people work for us."

"With money, we can buy anything," Marcus sighed.

"What's the one thing money can't buy?" Derek asked.

Marcus scratched and then shook his head.

"Time," Derek said raising his voice. "Money can't buy time. Can you buy back the times you lost while in jail all 'dem years? That's why I say we have to start this shit now, because we don't have much time to waste thinking about doing this shit!"

Marcus leaned over the gate and veered over at the view of the Manhattan skyline. His future was going nowhere and here comes this opportunity of a life time that could make him.

"I want to start my own record label, Marcus," Derek said. "I have the paper work ready I just need the down payment to get the studio and the second hand equipment."

Marcus slightly nodded his head while staring at the Empire State Building.

"Music and entertainment is pretty much the only avenue to walk, for black men like us." Derek paused and joined Marcus leaning over the gate looking ahead. "We can launch our own label together, but we need a start – a down payment, and that's what this is about, getting that initial capital. Everyday niggas be stopping me trying to sell me some homemade mix tape they made, looking to get out of the ghetto like we are; and some of these nigga got talent, too. I'm saying we can sign cats to our label an' shit. You see Marcus, the white man isn't going to give us an opportunity; we have to create one for ourselves my brotha. The system will fuck you if you're poor! It's time to fuck back."

Marcus turned his head to look at the other bridge connecting Brooklyn to Manhattan but noticed the waning gibbous moon shinning between the Twin Towers.

"You know," Marcus said. "I was walking home earlier today and you see 'dem same characters walking about being a part of the system, selling drugs to each other for a fucking pair of Jordans and a gold chain. None of them nigga ever decided to pool their money together and get the fuck out of the hood."

"You see, that's the difference between them and us," Derek said, hitting his friend on the side of the shoulders. "I mean you have dude driving BMWs and living in the projects, what the fuck! They're not building nothing, we will!" Derek exclaimed. "And while we at it, we might want to rob their asses too."

Marcus laughed.

"We can do this. Those Koreans come in to our community and take our money and build their shit in their community, and leave us dry; not anymore."

"I hear you, brotha."

"So, do I have a partner?" Derek sternly asked.

Marcus sighed and closed his eyes.

"Remember, you are doing this for your daughter's future, so she won't' have to deal with these hood niggas."

"I don't have a choice, what else is there," Marcus said looking down at the floor.

"You have a choice and you made the right one. We'll meet again and plan this shit out with Carter."

CHAPTER NINE

The conversation on the bridge gave some solace to Marcus who at the time was at the edge of a total meltdown. It was ironic that crime was the only way out when it was crime that brought him where he is now. This opportunity that Derek presented would pull him out of the abyss in which he was born into. Marcus thought about the men in his housing project who are rich from their underworld activities, but yet poor. How can that be, he thought. These men easily pull in thousands of dollars a day in one housing unit alone, but still live in one of the worst residential section of New York City. Where's that money going and to whom? When and if this is all over, most of these men will still be living at Marcy; and so will their children.

Marcy generates more money per week, from the crack enterprise, than most major corporations do, but yet it's still the ghetto of Bedford Stuyvesant. How is that possible? Who is behind the crack cocaine operation? Marcus was determined to find out who was at the top of the food chain as far as Marcy was concerned. That would be difficult and dangerous for one person but for three people it may be possible.

The phone rang in the kitchen, and Marcus was able to get it before his mother came rushing out of her bedroom.

"Hello."

"Yo, it's Carter, how you doing?"

"Hey Carter," Marcus said as he became nervous. He could hear his own heart racing. He hoped Carter didn't hear it either. "I'm good."

"We gon' meet at the barber shop, I'm going to close up instead."

"Are we going to talk about…"

"Yeah, we go'na talk about the plan."

"Ok, I'll be there tonight."

"Good. Bye."

As Marcus made his way to the barber shop, it occurred to him that the armed robbery attempt that got him in jail the last time didn't involve anyone being killed. That would be something that he will have to bring forward when discussing the plan with the other two. Murder is not an option at this point. Marcus was not planning on spending the rest of his life in jail for a few thousands of dollars. This would have to be a clean getaway without anyone getting hurt or God forbid killed.

Marcus became more accepting of Derek's idea. He was desperate for money, so desperate, that the thought of robbing someone on the subway or even robbing a bodega had cross his mind a couple of times. He had no weapon, but he could always get a fake gun and hope he would never have to use it as a real one.

"Yo, Marcus," Carter said to him as he entered the barber shop.

"Come on over here, bro," Derek said gesturing for Marcus to sit next to him. "We don't got time to waste, yo."

The two were sitting in the back of the barber shop, around a small table. The shop had already closed for the day.

It was late, it was pass ten o'clock and the owner had left and partially closed up for the day. Derek had a pen and paper already out and was engaging in a conversation with Carter when Marcus walked over to the back area of the shop.

"Yo pull up a chair," Derek said. "There's one right over there." Derek pointed to the half broken chair that was lying next to the radiator against the wall. "All right, listen," he continued. "We got to do this shit right, there is no room for failure…"

"Can I ask a quick question," Marcus interrupted. "Don't we need guns?"

"Yeah, I got that taken care of," Derek answered. "We'll discuss that in a minute."

"Good, because I was about to say," Marcus replied.

"I used to date a sista who used to work in the place about a few months ago and she told me that they have a safe in the basement where they keep the money at."

"You still keep in touch with this woman?" Carter asked.

"Nah, she lives in Newark with her sister, now," Derek said as he pulled out a cigarette. "Haven't spoken to her since she left Brooklyn. Anyway, she saw the safe by accident when the boss's wife loss her engagements ring. She was told to help find it. She went down the steps to the basement and noticed a safe, placed in the corner away from everything else. But it was hidden behind a shelf. You would never notice it, she said, if you weren't looking for something. She also told me that the boss has another business somewhere else and keeps the cash from that business in the safe also."

"Was she trying to take money from the safe?" Carter asked.

"Probably, that's why she knew about all this shit," Derek laughed. "You see, that's where all our money in the community goes. Working class people here in Bed-Stuy cash their checks, social security checks, and are charged high ass rates just to cash a fucking check!"

"There's no other place people can go, too," said Marcus. "There's no other check cashing place around the area."

"The one going up near Bushwick is owned by Asians too," said Carter.

"Well, it's time for us to get a piece of the pie," Derek exclaimed. "Twice a month an armored truck comes and replenish whatever cash is need. So, the best time to hit them would be the day after the truck delivers cash to them."

"The safe is just about full by then?" Carter asked.

"Correct!" Derek yelled.

"So how do we get in?" Marcus asked.

Derek began drawing a diagram of the layout of the store on a piece of paper he had layout on the table.

"Over here," Derek said, pointing to a section of the diagram. "At the back of the store is an entrance to the basement. I will pose as an utility worker. I have an old Con Edison jacket and badge that my brother left at the house when is left the company a few years ago. I will make my way in before the store opens at Eight O'clock, through the front entrance. This is before the employees come in for work."

"They won't let you in," Carter said shaking his head.

"They will," Derek confidentially spoke. "I will call the business from a pay phone the day before and let them know that Con Ed needs to reexamine their meter for a possible upgrade. Remember, there was a small black out in that area not too long ago."

"Yeah, I remember it," Marcus said. "It was only a few hours during the day, though."

"Yeah, I know but I can use that as an excuse along with the company jacket, a fake badge and some disguise I bought from some Halloween store on Fulton."

"What yo ass going to be wearing a mask?" Marcus laughed.

"Nah, like a fake beard, and some thick glasses and some other shit," Derek said.

"Ok, so what about us, when do we come in?" Carter asked.

"Carter you will be a look out and back up," Derek looked at Carter while pointing at the diagram. "But you'll be outside on the sidewalk near the back entrance, because that's where we are going to exist and that's where you'll park the car, half way down the block. Marcus, when I get in, and I'm down in the basement I will have the owner open the back door to let you in. Marcus, I will make him open the safe while you deal with the wife if she's there or any other problems that may arise."

"Yeah, man, I can do that, but will I have a gun also?" Marcus asked.

"I may not be able to get you or Carter one, but I'll have a metal pipe or a knife or something like that for you."

Marcus seemed at little nervous about the whole operation. A series of thoughts flowed in his mind. What if the owners didn't cooperate and tries to escape or something. What if he or Derek had to use deadly force at some point?

"If the owner gets out of line we may have to…" Marcus began speaking.

"Don't worry about that man, this is simple," Derek said trying to reassure the other two. "Once they see the gun in my hand, they will cooperate, trust me!"

"When are you going to do this?" Marcus asked.

"This Friday," Derek answered sharply. "The armored truck delivers on Thursday."

Derek began to get out of his chair while the other two followed.

"By the way, fellas, I was told that they always arrive at the store at least an hour before opening. We need to be there shortly after then, before the workers get there, understand?"

"Yeah," the other two said.

"I will call each of you guys in the morning on Friday and you will meet me in front of St. Bethel Baptist Church not too far from Marcy and I will pick you up from there."

CHAPTER TEN

It was Friday morning and Marcus never slept the whole night. His body ached from the twist and turns that kept him up. There was a dull headache in his temples and forehead caused by tension and worrying about the next day.

It was the big day, and he waited for the phone to ring. The anxiety was unbearable and excruciating. He was gripped by fear. He felt like he was being pulled from both sides. On one hand he was finally going to get the money he needed to jump start his life, but on the other hand there was the possibility of getting caught. Taking short cuts in life was not something he wanted to do, but that was a gamble that the system impelled the average black man to do. It was the only escape out of no way out. He thought of cancelling the event. That thought crossed his mind throughout the night and into the very moment. "Man, I'm not going to fucking go," Marcus exclaimed to himself. Then the phone rang.

"Hello," Marcus said with a very faint voice. He could barely get the word out of his mouth. He felt his heart hammering at his chest like a drum. Each beat vibrated throughout his body, with beads of sweat rolling down his back. He could barely keep his knees straight.

"Let's do this, meet me at the church in fifteen minutes,"

it was Derek's voice and he hung up the phone without saying another word.

The moment was here. He took a deep breath and exhaled slowly. He grabbed a pair of jeans that was lying on a pile of clothes behind the sofa. A hoodie was lying there too, along with a pair of sneakers; he put them on as well and headed down the stairs and into the streets.

The streets were calm at this time of the morning. The usual characters were not present; they had retired for the night and are asleep. The sun had just pierced the horizon and the cool scent of the morning breeze provided a tranquility that was badly needed at the very moment.

Marcus walked up Nostrand Avenue pass the subway station and strolled around the corner. He spotted a coffee shop a block from the church. Coffee was a dollar fifty, shamefully, he could barely afford it. He had seven dollars in his wallet, but he should see much more by the end of the day, he thought with a smile.

He carefully adjusted his hood to hide his face from the lone customer and the clerk. After leaving the store, with coffee in hand, he spotted a car up ahead and across the street from the church, with dark smoke fuming from the exhaust pipe. Halfway through finishing his coffee, he spotted a bearded man with a baseball cap and a pair of shade behind the wheel of an old and run-down Buick Oldsmobile.

"I almost didn't recognize you, man," Marcus said opening the front passenger side door.

"You wasn't supposed to," Derek replied as he adjusted a gun that was underneath his denim shirt but tucked slightly below his waist band.

"Carter ain't come yet?"

"Finish your coffee," Derek sternly said. "He's patrolling the area before we get there."

"You think you can handle this?" Derek asked.

"Yeah, I'm good...it is what it is, you know," Marcus said nervously as he took his final sips of the coffee.

The car drove off and Marcus quickly discarded his empty cup of coffee out of the side window.

"You know Derek," Marcus said. "I was thinking to myself on the way here and I asked myself, 'Why am I doing this?'".

"Your answer is you have nothing to lose," Derek said turning to his friend who was feeling doubtful. "I just saved you the energy of having to come up with the answer yourself, you can thank me later." Derek made a sharp turn at a corner. "You're probably better off in jail, Marcus, than where you are now...I'm I lying?"

Marcus turned his face away from his friend and thought about the Manhattan skyline that he saw on the Williamsburg Bridge. It was the very first time he ever got a chance to view Manhattan from that stand point, it made an impression on him.

"Nigga, you don't got two nickels to rub together, so shut the fuck up and let's do this shit," Derek insisted.

The two men didn't exchange further words to each other until they spotted Carter walking towards them wearing a black baseball cap and a black leather jacket.

"Yo Carter," Derek yelled at Carter who was walking towards the car. "Get behind the wheels and keep the engine running and move the car further down near the end of the block."

"I'll wait near the back entrance, right?" Marcus said as his friend surveyed the area slowly with his eyes.

Derek noticed the owner's car parked in the back near the rear entrance.

"Sounds good, just be careful and don't look too

suspicious," Derek said as he placed a duffle bag over his shoulders. "Matter of fact, walk half way down the block and come back, by the time you get back I should have had the back door open for you."

Derek headed to the front entrance of the check cashing and money transfer store. Sun light had just kicked in and his natural disguise was fading quickly. There was no time to waste. The metal gate was little more than half open and he banged on the glass door. An Asian man appeared through the back behind the bullet proof barrier. Derek could see doubt in his eyes. A look of uncertainty and vulnerability bestowed him at that moment. Derek displayed his badge and shifted his jacket so the man could see the logo of the electric company on his jacket.

"I'm from Con Ed," Derek said faintly. "We have an appointment; sorry I arrive a little early. May I come in?"

The man briefly turned around and looked as if he was speaking to someone. Moments later he walked to the front door and Derek showed his badge to the man who seemed a little reluctant to let him in.

The man opened the door. "Hi," he said. "You from Con Edison?"

"You may need an upgrade, right?" Derek said nervously as the man slowly moved out of the way.

Derek tried real hard to avoid making eye contact with the owner in hope that he may not see his intentions in his eyes. As Derek walked to the open door pass the bullet proof barrier, he discreetly looked around to see who the man was talking to. It was his wife, who was sitting down eating breakfast from a bowl.

"Down the stairs, right?" Derek asked, but sounded like a statement.

"Yes," the owner opened the trap door which displayed

the stairs that lead to the basement.

They both walked down the stairs. The owner clicked on a light switch and proceeded to the location of the meter. Derek saw the door that led to the outside where Marcus should be by now, and walked over to it.

"I need you to open this door," Derek said quietly.

"Excuse me?" the owner asked narrowing his eyes. "What for?"

Derek reached into his waist band and pulled out a .22 millimeter pistol and pointed it at the owner who stared dumbfounded at him.

"Open the fucking door!" Derek looked him dead in the eye. "Don't say a word and you and your wife won't get hurt, understood?"

The owner nodded his head fearfully.

"Now open the door," Derek said pointing to the back entrance.

The owner pulled the latches located on the top and bottom of the door. Marcus quickly pushed the door open almost knocking the owner to the floor. Both Derek and Marcus stood in front of the owner in the dim lit room.

"What do you guys want?" the owner asked.

"You know what we want," Marcus said, adjusting the ski mask on his face.

"I don't know," the owner said furiously looking back and forth at both men.

"Where's the money...the safe muthafucka!" Derek exclaimed quietly.

"There's no safe here, what do you mean?"

Marcus grabbed the owner by the neck and pushed him up against the concrete wall causing his head to hit the wall.

"Where's the fucking safe, nigga!" Marcus became angry still squeezing his neck.

"We don't got time," Derek began looking around for it. "Here it is fucking liar! Now open it. Bring him over here."

The commotion stopped when they heard the owner's wife saying something in Korean.

"Tell her to come down here," Derek pointing the gun at the owner who was on the ground struggling to get away from Marcus. Derek walked over and struck the owner on the side of his head with the butt of the gun. "Tell her to come down here, now."

The owner quickly yelled something in Korean and his wife slowly walked down the stairs. Derek quickly grabbed the wife by the hair and forced her down the stair as she screamed helplessly trying to free herself from his grip. Holding the gun with one hand he pulled her hair downward forcing her to sit on the floor.

"Yo, make him open the safe," Derek said looking at Marcus. "God damn it!"

"I'm trying," Marcus said to Derek while dragging the owner over to where the safe was. "Now open the fucking safe, and hurry the fuck up!"

The owner instinctively wiped the blood off of the side of his head and reached for the knob. "It's locked," he mumbled. "Please don't hurt me."

"Unlock it then," Derek shouted from across the room while choking the owner's wife from behind with his arms around her neck as she cried silently.

"I don't remember the combination," the owner said. "I ...really don't."

"Nigga, you better remember that shit," said Derek dragging the wife across the floor with his hand around her neck.

"Stop playing games," Marcus said as he became furious. "Open the fucking safe, yo."

Shaken and breathing heavily for air, the owner turned and looked over at his wife crying hysterically.

"I know something that will refresh his fucking memory," Derek said while reaching for the gun in his waist. Derek pointed the gun at the wife's head. "Now I give you fucking Koreans three second to come up with the combination."

The owner's wife began screaming hysterically, trying desperately to free herself from Derek's grip. Suddenly, the owner started turning the combination wheel on the safe. His first attempt failed!

"Try again, muthafucka!" Marcus yelled in his ear as he whipped the owner's sweat from his hand.

"I'm trying," the owner said turning the wheel while gazing at the number on it. Sweat began to trickle off of his head and created a damp spot on the back of his shirt. He began to cough as he desperately tries to remember the combination.

His second attempt failed again to produce any results.

"You sonofabitch!" Marcus yelled. "Keep trying, keep trying!"

The owner's wife continued to scream and plead as Derek choked her and finally lifted her up on her feet and threw her to the ground. The owner looked in horror as his wife cried out to him in Korean. Derek quickly hits her in the forehead with the butt of the gun causing her to fade briefly into unconsciousness.

"I'm ma gon ask you again, open the damn safe," Derek looked sternly at the owner; his voice was soft and intense.

The owner began turning the wheel on the safe, he turned it to the right, he turned it to the left, and to the right again and stopped. He whipped the sweat from his brow and slowly grabbed the handle and pushed downward; it gave way, the door opened.

"Damn, fuck!" a sigh of relief engulfed Marcus who displayed a smile of joy. The room was quiet and motionless for a brief moment as the two men anticipate what was hidden inside the mini vault. Marcus swiftly dragged the owner out of the way and the two men huddled around the safe.

"I didn't bring a flash light, oh well," Derek said as he reached into the safe with his right hand. He pulled out a large redweld envelope. He untied the string and flipped the cover. "Oh shit!"

There were stacks of twenties, fifties, tens, fives, and singles, all wrapped separately. The men froze when a black bag was pulled out from the back of the safe containing all hundreds; small stacks of them. Marcus did not recognize the man's face on the bills. It was the first time he ever saw a hundred dollar bill. The scent of crisp hundred dollar bills created a sense of nostalgia. They had finally made it. For once in their lives they felt they beat the system.

Suddenly, they heard someone marching up the stairs. It was the owner's wife who was making her way up the stairs to the main floor. Trying to catch her balance, she grabbed the railing and pulled herself up the steep staircase while she climbed higher and higher.

"Marcus, quick!" Derek yelled.

Marcus ran towards the stairs, leaped, and grabbed her by her dress just before she made it to the top and was able to pull her down with his weight and caused her to fall several flights to the cement floor. She fell head first.

"Oh, no," Marcus said almost apologetically, as he notice blood oozing from the back of her head which had produce a loud thump as it hit the floor. "Fuck!"

A struggle ensued between Derek and the owner, who was on top of Derek punching him. He then managed to get his hands around Derek's neck, squeezing it with all his might.

Marcus didn't notice the commotion that was going on, on the other side of the room. Derek was unable to speak or shout for that manner. Derek was slowly losing consciousness. Marcus, who was regretfully staring over the pool of blood, was jolted by the sound of a gunshot. Derek had managed to pull his weapon from his waist and fired a shot. The owner was seen lying on the floor flickering his eye lids and holding the side of his abdomen.

"Don't leave me to die," was last heard from the owner, as the two men quickly grabbed the two items of money and eased their way through the back door.

The two men walked up the street with their heads slightly tiled downward. Marcus had taken off his mask and began whipping off the sweat that was dripping off his face and neck. The block was virtually empty, except for the car that was waiting for them up the block.

"No one had seem us leave, it was easy money, it was better than selling crack on the street corner waiting to get shot by a rival gang member who would just see us as another nigga in the hood," Derek joyfully said as he adjusted the folder under his arm.

As they walked up the street they saw Carter waiting in the driver's seat.

"How'd it go?" Carter asked putting the car in drive. "That's a big envelope."

"Let's get the fuck outta here," Derek commanded as he got in the front seat. "I hope no one saw you standing here."

"Nah," Carter said. "I had to take a piss though."

"What," Derek replied shockingly. "You left the car…I told you…never mind."

"Are we going to the barber shop," Carter asked.

"I tell you guys what," Derek started to say. "I need to take the car back to the person I borrowed it from. Why don't

I meet you guys at the barber shop later tonight with the money?"

"No," Marcus objected. "Let split this shit up now."

"Carter can stay late like last time," Derek stated. "And close up after we're done."

"Nigga, we just killed two people back there, and you won't give me my money?" Marcus became furious at his friend.

"Claim the fuck down, man," Derek exclaimed. "You'll get your money."

"I'm driving to the barber shop," Carter stated as he made a right turn. "Doc ain't there yet, I got the keys, I can open the doors for us and we can count the money in the back."

The three men pulled up to the barber shop where they spent an hour counting and distributing the money amongst themselves. Derek took the lion share. They had plans to meet up again to discuss starting their own record label.

Marcus left the barber shop with a bag of money stashed under his shirt. However, he wasn't quite happy. It was the first time he ever killed someone. Then again, it was an accident, he thought to himself. "If she hadn't run up the stair, all of it wouldn't have happened," he said out loud as he headed home. It was her fault; he tried to reassure himself that he didn't murder anyone. Marcus had his money in a paper bag. He had over $15,000 dollars' worth of cash on him. It was more money than he ever dreamed of possessing in a million years.

As he made his way down Myrtle Avenue, he thought about paying off the child support money he owed. This new venture would be his one-way ticket out of the hood.

As he got closer to the housing units, he could see a configuration of youths forming a circle and cheering. It's not unusual to see people fighting in and around the projects.

Most people ignore them unless someone is stabbed, shot, or dies as a result of the conflict. This gathering seemed different. As Marcus got closer he noticed a young man doing what appears to be freestyle rapping. He was a slender youth in his early twenties. He had a slim built. He was wearing a NY Knicks basketball jersey, with a short afro that was freshly cut. He used a lot of hand gesture when he rapped to get his point across. The crowd was very much into what he was rapping about. Some people in the crowd were egging him on saying "tear that shit up". One of the young men which Marcus recognized as a known drug dealer started making beat sounds with his mouth. Marcus was never exposed to the rap culture while in prison, but what he was witnessing before his eyes was new to him, moreover, fascinating. Minutes later, another rapper came out from the woodworks, after the other one finished. He was a heavy set teen who sported a flat top hair style. He was less aggressive than the other youth but not as appealing to most of the people who were watching. The two men were basically battling each other through words. Marcus liked what he saw and decided he would speak with one of the men.

Rap Music and its industry served three purposes for the youth at Marcy. First, it provided a means of escape from the mental effects of poverty and depression. Second, it provided a means of employment for young men who had no future in corporate America because of a lack of a formal education. Thirdly, it provided a platform for youths to express their frustration with institutional racism and political and economic oppression.

As the group of youth dispersed, Marcus approached the youngster who he first saw rapping. The young man celebrated his victory, briefly with some of his other colleagues. Marcus saw potential, energy, and promise from the young man. He waited until he departed from a young girl who he was talking to, before approaching him.

"Excuse me," Marcus said politely.

"What's going on?" the young man replied.

"I heard you rapping there, and I must say homie, you were pretty good."

"Thanks."

"Listen, you ever thought about going further in this rapping thing you got going on?"

"What do you mean, I just like doing it, you know."

"I understand, but, you ever thought about recording a song?"

"Yeah, I just never knew where to go or who to see," the young man said. "But yeah, that would be cool. You a hip hop producer or something?"

"I have a friend who's a producer and he's looking for new talent. He, in fact, just started a new record label."

The two men walked to the end of the corner. The building where he lived was adjacent to where Marcus lived. Marcus noticed ambition in the young man's demeanor. He was different from the other youth he met at Marcy. He seemed more introverted and a little shy; however, it was what kept him out of trouble. There was something different about this youth; he did not belong in the hood. He had the potential to make it out and escape from Marcy.

"My home boys and I are trying to get together a record label and we could use some new talent."

"Oh shit, I can do that," the young man became excited. "So I can make my own album?"

"Yeah, exactly," Marcus said. "By the way, what's your name?"

"They call me Joe-Joe."

"One Joe ain't good enough," Marcus laughed.

"My real name is Joe or Joseph," the young man continued. "When I was younger and my mother called me, she would say Joe twice, in case I didn't hear the first Joe; then people thought that was my name and started calling me Joe-Joe, thinking that was my name."

"I see, that's interesting," Marcus said. "My name, by the way, is Marcus."

Joe-Joe nodded his head.

"How old are you Joe-Joe?"

"Nineteen."

"Joe-Joe, I been out of the scene for a couple of years...actually thirteen...How's the hip hop scene like now?"

"Well, there's a new group in Los Angeles doing gangsta rap, is what they call it," Joe-Joe smiled and eagerly continued. "It's a little more hardcore than what is here on the east coast. There's a lot of free styling goin' on in other projects like in Queens and the Bronx. Hip hop is growing and one day I believe it will make niggas like you and me who grow up in the projects, millionaires."

"I find it hard that anybody from Marcy can make it to super stardom," Marcus said scratching the back of his head. "From what I'm seeing you're the realist nigga I've met since coming back to Marcy, for real though."

"Nah, there's a lot of cool niggas around, it's just that everyone has to play their role to survive in the hood, know what I'm sayin'. Like myself, most of these niggas never been outside the hood. The only reality they know is the ghetto and that's all about surviving, nothing else...that's all it is for them. Hip hop is a way for me and other youths to mentally step outside the ghetto in order to survive it." Joe-Joe stopped to look at a police car that drove by. "I go to hip hop when I want to escape from Marcy. I use it like how people around here uses crack."

At the sound of these words that he was hearing, Marcus was amazed. Where had those words come from? Marcus tried to hide his shocked expression. He couldn't wait to tell Derek about his new discovery.

"What type of rapping do you do?" Marcus asked.

"Conscious rap is what they call it," Joe-Joe exclaimed. "It deals more with social issues, than just fuckin' niggas up, and fuckin' bitches, you know what I mean."

"I definitely know what you mean, bro."

Marcus adjusted the bag of money under his arm. "Tell me how come you haven't got mixed up selling crack an' shit like all these other dudes?"

"I used be a runner for a couple of dudes around here at one time, though," Joe-Joe added. "But sometimes they may ask me to do it from time to time. I need the money, you know? Sometimes you just get tired of eating corn flakes for dinner and you do what cha got to do."

"I understand," Marcus said. "Be careful those niggas can set you up."

"Marcus, I got to go," Joe-Joe said. "I just remembered my mom is expecting me."

"I don't have a pen, to give you my number…"

"It's all right; I'm always out here, out on the street somewhere."

"Cool, until we meet again. Peace."

When Marcus made his way up stairs, his mother was not home, so he had the apartment to himself to count his share of the money. He counted $16,440.

CHAPTER ELEVEN

Marcus was awakened by a conversation coming from the hallway outside the apartment front door. He recognized the voice of his neighbor. She was talking to his mother. After a short visit to the bathroom, Marcus quickly walked to the front to see what the hysteria was all about. When he got there, there were two other neighbors present.

"Marcus, my dear!" his mother said as she wiped the tears from her eyes, slowly grabbing her son. "This place is getting worst everyday damn day."

"Why, what happened?" Marcus asked looking at each person worriedly.

"Didn't you hear," she said frantically. "There was a killing at the check cashing place down the street. They robbed the check cashing place on Nostrand Avenue. They murdered the Korean man and his wife."

Marcus became numb from the revelation. He could hardly hear anything else she said after that. He could feel his blood pulsating through his vein. A panic engulfed him, and his breathe became shallow, but he had to play it off and pretend it's the first time he is hearing about it.

"They said the workers found them down in the basement," a neighbor said.

"All the money in the safe is gone," another neighbor said.

"Who could have done such a thing," his mother interjected. "Freaking animals, that's what they are."

"It must be someone from the projects, I bet," someone said.

"If it is, then they must be long gone by now," Marcus manage to outer.

"That's where I go to cash my social security check, too," a neighbor stated.

Marcus wanted to leave; he didn't want anyone to notice the distress in his eyes. He tried to avoid eye contact with anyone of the neighbors. The sweat from his brow and neck became more visible, as the conversation continued. As long as there were no witnesses that saw them at the place, they were good for now, he thought.

Two months have passed since the shooting incident at the check cashing store. There's been little activity except for detectives asking question to a few of the people in the neighborhood. There are posters, however, posted on the walls and trees throughout the neighborhood of Bed-Stuy for the arrest and capture of those who were involved in the death of the owners. Whenever Marcus would walk by one of those posters, it would give him chills throughout his entire body. It was something he had to put aside. He had to focus on the record label.

With the money that was obtained, the three men were able to start their own label. They called it *Dynasty Records*. They had obtained a lawyer to handle the legal work involved, and rented out a room in a store basement, in Bushwick, and used it as a studio. The studio wasn't like the fancy Manhattan ones they saw in magazines with a large waiting area, leather sofas, Jacuzzi, and a guest room for VIPs equipped with a HiFi stereo system and lounge area. Although slightly renovated with partitions and a new bathroom, it was simple and comfortable for the purposes of producing a first hit single. They bought second-hand recording and sampling equipment and some used furniture, and even hired a recording technician to assist with music production and mixing. They were ready to make money and accomplish what no one amongst their peers had ever done. They had signed Joe-Joe to the label and made him their first recording artist.

They started producing Joe-Joe's first single. They had the beat and they sampled music from other established and famous artist. Joe-Joe had the lyrics written out and memorized; it was just a matter of coalescing it all together to create a hit. A hit was what they needed to solidify their accomplishment. They were competing against other well-known artist in the New York area; some came from Long Island, while others had their roots in Hollis, Queens, but Brooklyn had to make its presents known. They were going to show the world what Brooklyn had to offer.

For Marcus, it was the birth of a new day. He was able to make payments on his child support now. He had told the judge that he was working for Derek as an assistant producer, and that Derek was the president and CEO of *Dynasty Records*. Derek even showed up at court and testified on his behalf. The judge was amazed and even thanked him for his tireless search for employment.

He mailed out his first payments to his baby mama, Thelma, along with back payments, which he took from his cut of the money almost leaving him high and dry with barely anything left over.

The death of the two owners no longer bothered Marcus. It no longer became a psychological hindrance in his life. It was as if the event never happened. He was too busy trying to assimilate his new life and the new single he was preparing to produce for the label. Everything was going well, except for one thing. It was Joe-Joe's mother.

Joe-Joe's mother found out what her son was doing during the evenings. She would tell him to "leaving them niggas alone", "You're waiting yo time with this gangsta bullshit!" She would scold him and tell him to look for a job at the Dominican owned supermarket down the block.

"I ain't gon' make no money working there, Ma," Joe-Joe said to his mother who was posing to smack him for talking back. "I can make more money doing this, besides the people on the block like my lyrics."

"Nigga, I don't care what other people say, that shit ain't paying the bills," his mother screamed. "Now go out there and work for somebody."

"I can rap, though."

"Ain't nobody listening to that crap!"

"Marcus is helping me to write a new song," Joe-Joe said to his mother.

"I don't care Joe-Joe, you need to get yo' self a real job and stop following that fool before you end up like that stupid brother of yours."

Marcus had tried to speak to Joe-Joe's mother with no avail. She cursed him out, called him a nigga, told him he wasn't a real man for not seeking a job somewhere at the local supermarket or the neighborhood drug store. It was pointless to pursue the matter anymore. Joe-Joe would lie and tell his mother he got a job working at the meat packing place on Myrtle Avenue. He told her he worked different shifts. This gave Joe-Joe a chance to record his new single.

Marcus was attracted to Joe-Joe's mother; she was a fine late thirty something, dark skin black female with a jet black weave that rolled down her back, and a set of well-toned legs to go with it. When she talked, she would gesture with her hands so everyone would see her long polished colored nails and freshly manicured fingers. She always wore tight spandex dresses which drew a lot of attention from the other fellas on the block. The attraction they had for each other created a sexual tension between the two which always led to an argument. It wasn't too long before Marcus would borrow Derek's car and drive the short distance back to her apartment while little Joe-Joe was in the studio recording. Marcus would argue with her about Joe-Joe. One time when she smacked Marcus in the face for calling her a stupid bitch, he cornered her in her son's bedroom, a struggle ensued and her tattooed up ass became exposed from his constant pulling on her white T-shirt. Marcus noticed that her ass bounced whenever she tried to free herself from his monstrous grip. That gave him no reason to let go of her shirt until part of her shirt tore. He could not stop his erection from developing; it was trapped in his pants like a snake wanting to be set free from its cage. She finally surrendered to his aggressive masculinity, her breath changed to a quick rapid gasp laced with a light and delicate moan. She was hungry and eager for it; Marcus could see it in her eyes. He threw her on the bed like a sack of dirty laundry. After removing his jean, his shirt and her underwear, Marcus stroked her with her legs wrapped around his lower back. Each push of his pelvis moving deeper and deeper into her brought her closer and closer to ecstasy. When Marcus was done, his shoulders would hurt from scratch marks and her constantly battering him with her fist.

"Joe-Joe's mother was not the type of woman to make love to," Marcus remembered telling Carter at their newly open studio. "She's the type you just fuck, she's a hood rat, and she can't appreciate the finer things in life, like candle light dinners and a quiet walk in the park. She would think you boring. Bitches like that like to be treated like bitches."

"Maybe if you treat her right, then she would want the finer things in life," Carter objected.

"That woman is a by-product of the hood. You can't change a hood rat into a housewife," Marcus excitedly stated. "Her mother was a hood rat, and that's the only way she knows how to treat a man is what she learned from her hood rat mama."

"How many times did you hit that?" Carter asked smiling.

"About four or five times, maybe six," Marcus tried to recall.

"One time, Joe-Joe almost caught us," Marcus said. "She was giving me head on the couch, we heard someone trying to open the front door, luckily Joe-Joe dropped his keys, and that gave me enough time to pull my pants up and act like nothing happened before he manage to unlock the door."

"He knows you banging his mom's?"

"Yeah, probably, who knows," Marcus said. "Joe-Joe only cares about making money right now and getting out of the hood." Marcus took a sip of the wine he was drinking. It was one of the left over celebration bottles, from when they first opened for business. "I tell you one thing, though; she knows how to give a mean blow job. If he didn't walk in the living room, I would have choked that bitch for sure."

It's been two weeks since Marcus last been to the studio. He received a call from Derek; Joe-Joe's single has been completed. The final editing was presented to Derek, by the recording technician, who listened to it and was amazed at what he heard. He wanted Marcus to come and listen to it before they send the final draft to a distributor who had promised to release the single if they felt it was worthy enough. The distributor was a prestigious record company in Manhattan. They jumped started a lot of careers in the music industry, including rappers from the west coast.

Marcus braved the late autumn weather; it was unusually cold for that time of the year. The streets were crowded with people coming from work. People on the streets were forced to walk a step faster to avoid the chilling breeze that was no match for their fall garments. They had been fooled by the warmer temperature earlier in the daytime.

When Marcus arrived at the studio, before he opened the door he could hear music playing; it had a steady bass sound with a synthesizer melody accompanying it. When he got inside, Joe-Joe was rapping behind the booth. He was wearing a dark gray hoodie sweater, fingerless gloves, and blue baggy jeans. Everyone else was already there including Derek, Carter, and the technician. The song had apparently just started before he walked in; it was rhythmic yet soothing. Joe-Joe rapped the lyrics:

> *It seems like there's no way out of this shit,*
> *No matter how hard you try,*
> *My Marcy brothers keep yo head up high,*
> *But don't reach for the sky,*
> *Because the sky is only an illusion,*
> *Created by satanic institutions,*
> *To support your own delusions,*
> *For manipulation and collusions.*
> *So look within but don't fit in,*
> *Or you bound to commit a grievous sin...*

Joe-Joe continued to rap the rest of the single.

When the song final ended Derek smiled and turned to Marcus and said, "I think this is it, bro."

"I think so to," Marcus joyfully replied grabbing Derek's shoulder. "Shit is dope."

Joe-Joe walked out of the booth and greeted everyone. The technician stated that this recording would be the final cut that they would give to the distributor in the city.

"Joe-Joe did you come up with a name for the song yet or do you want us to name it?" the technician asked Joe-Joe.

"I wan'na call it '*No Way Out*'," Joe-Joe said nodding his head.

"Why that name?" Derek asked stroking his chin and leaning back in his chair.

"I want to dedicate it to my sister who died a year ago."

"Why, what happened," Carter looked surprised.

He had everyone's attention in the room. Marcus had heard that his sister had died but never inquired about it from his mother.

"She and two other dudes robbed this nigga who ended up being a crack dealer in the other project," Joe-Joe cleared his throat. "A couple of weeks later she ended up trying to buy crack from the same guy who recognized her. Someone found her on the ground with two shots to her side, she died at the hospital."

Marcus and Derek quickly looked at each other and turned away.

"Do you know where that guy is?" Carter asked.

"Yeah, he's in jail," Joe-Joe replied.

"Ok, so why '*No Way Out*'?" Derek asked again.

"There's no way out of this bitch, you know!" Joe-Joe exclaimed as he raised his arms and violently dropped them. "The whole system is like a fucking prison. Everybody I know who tried to leave Marcy always end up dead. Stabbed, shot, you name it…I'm sick of it!"

The room became completely silent; everyone froze like the world had stopped turning. For a moment no one said a word until Derek stood up from his chair.

"Don't worry son, this song, is your one way ticket out of this bitch hole," Derek laughed shamefully as he walked over to Joe-Joe. "Soon you and your mom's will be living large in the suburbs somewhere."

"I hope so," Joe-Joe said.

"Let's get outta here, I'm going to take this to the record company first thing in the morning," Derek said, speaking like a corporate executive at a board meeting. "Joe-Joe, I want you to come with me tomorrow morning so you can take a few photograph for the cover. I will pick you up and we'll drive there."

Joe-Joe agreed and they all left for the day.

Later that day Derek informed the group that the executives loved the song and was willing to distribute and market the single on the FM radio stations throughout New York and the rest of the country. The song would be sold to the public as a single in cassette form as well as a limited vinyl production; in addition, they signed a contract with Dynasty Records to have Joe-Joe record an album with a least eight songs which would include his single 'No Way Out'. Joe-Joe was excited about the new project. The news couldn't have been better.

Joe-Joe spent most of his time writing in his notebook, writing down words that rhymed with each other. It wasn't easy, but he had an obligation to fulfill, fast. Everywhere he was seen, he had his notebook with him. Sometimes a catchy phrase would enter his mind; he had to stop and quickly write it down before it escaped his mind. Once when he was asleep and dreaming in bed, he heard a tone in his dream; he jumped out of bed in the middle of the night, to write down the chorus that he heard in his dream. He then realized what woke him in the first place. It was a loud noise coming from outside the building. He opened and peeped out of his bedroom window to see what the commotion was that was taken place outside out on the sidewalk near his first floor apartment. A teenager and man in his mid-twenties were arguing loudly over an exchange gone bad, it appeared. Moments later after a brief exchange of words, the teenage swung a punch that landed on the other man's left side of his face. The young man staggered for a few seconds, almost falling to the ground before he was able to catch his balance by hitting the side of a parked car. His jaw became swollen, and blood became apparent as he tried to wipe it from his mouth with the sleeve of his shirt.

"Where's my shit!" the young man yelled.

"I don't owe you nutin' nigga," the teenager replied angrily. "Get the fuck outta here before I drop you bitch!"

"But I'm still standing, though," the young man said stretching his arms to the side. "I ate that punch, nigga, that's all you got…so was' up."

The young man began approaching the teenager with a clenched fist as onlookers strolled by to see what was happening. Lights from the other apartments in the complex began to come on, as more people woke up to see what was taken place. The young man moved closer to the teenager with his arm stretched out, cursing at the top of his lungs. Instantly, the teenager can be seen pulling out a gun from under his shirt; a shock filled the air, two shots rang out, and the young man ran swiftly, dodging through parked vehicles, and was seen running down the block until he disappeared out of sight. The teenager quickly left the scene.

Joe-Joe was a little surprise, but not at all shocked, at what he just experience. Even after the incident, a number of people was still roaming outside, on this early cold December night. Some of the residents were seen walking on the sidewalk without a coat or sweater, apparently looking for their next hit, unshaken by the event that just transpired. When Joe-Joe went back to his bed to write down what he had heard in his sleep, he couldn't remember it. "Fuck," he exclaimed. "These brain dead muthafuckin' niggas made me lose my song again!" Joe-Joe angrily threw his notebook against the wall and cursed the housing project. "Why am I still here," he screamed. "Fuck this place!" With all the distractions that had taken place, Joe-Joe's song was forever lost in his head.

It's been a week since Joe-Joe's single has been released to the public, and Marcus was to meet the other two at the studio. As Marcus left his apartment, and traveled down Myrtle Avenue, he heard a song coming from someone's car; it sounded pretty familiar. As the car drove closer to him, he almost went into shock. It was Joe-Joe's song playing on a car radio. He quickly ran over to the car which stopped at a red light and waved at the man inside, who was wearing a black Kangol hat and smoking a cigar. The man smiled and bopped his head to the rhythm of the beat while quietly looking at Marcus who was standing at the curb listening to the song blasting from the car radio.

"New song, huh," the man said looking at Marcus near the passenger side of his car.

"That's my song," Marcus said.

"Mine's too," the man replied.

"No," Marcus objected. "I mean, I produced the song."

"What?" the man said surprisingly. "Are you fucking kidding me?"

"Hell, nah," Marcus walked closer to the car. "His name is Joe-Joe, the rapper you hear sing."

"Oh, is that right?"

"Yeah, I'm a producer...I work for the owner of the label that he's signed to."

"Well congratulation. I wish you and him great success," the man said holding the cigar to his mouth.

"Thanks," Marcus said while reaching in his pocket. "Here's our business card, call us if you know someone who has talent and may want to sign to our label."

A horn could be heard honking from behind the car indicating that the traffic signal had changed. "I gotta go," the driver said. "But I will defiantly give a call if I hear anything, aight man."

Marcus continued his journey only to find a poster of Joe-Joe on the side glass window of a hair salon. It had a picture of Joe-Joe wearing his hooded sweater with his arms cross in front of his chest. In the background was a picture of the Marcy apartment buildings. The name of the single was written on the poster. Marcus was impressed. He was able to catch a gypsy cab to Broadway. The cab was almost full; he virtually had to squeeze his way into the passenger rear back seat as the lady next to him reluctantly moved to the center. As the cab quickly rushed through traffic, up ahead, he notice a poster, it was a poster of Joe-Joe, for the promotion of his new single on a transit bus. The bus flew by going in the opposite direction. Marcus quickly turned around just in time to quickly get a view of it. He bumped into the woman sitting next to him, who swiftly let him know that he didn't say, "excuse me". Marcus became overwhelmed with joy, pride, and satisfaction at what he was seeing. He could not believe how quickly his life was turning around. Not too long ago his life was about to fall off of a cliff; now he is on the verge of becoming a millionaire. He could not contain himself. "Sorry but that my nigga, Joe-Joe, we just made a hit song," Marcus said out loud.

"You know that rapper?" the woman next to him asked.

"Yeah, I helped produce the single," Marcus said excitingly.

"I was listening to it with my daughter his morning," the woman said. "She bought the cassette last night at the record store on Fulton Street. It's definitely popping. He must be new, I never heard him before?"

The young man in the passenger seat leaned over to his left and said, "I bought the cassette too, it's a cool song, it's a little bit more poetic than the other rap songs I've heard in the past couple of months. "Is he working on an album?"

"Matter of fact, I'm going to the studio right now to work on his new songs for his album," Marcus said as he smiled.

The other passengers and the driver exchanged words with Marcus until his stop came. The cab came to a stop as the young man in the front signaled the drive to stop at the corner. The man got out of the cab and thanked Marcus, and wished him good luck. It was the first time Marcus felt like he had a destination in his life. It was no more surviving by chance, or begging his mother for money. He was about to be his own man and experience some degree of independence for the first time in his life. For once in his life, he felt a weight lifted off his shoulders. He felt he was has free as an eagle.

He arrived at the studio, to see balloons, ribbons, and fake hundred dollar bills hanging from the walls and ceiling. In the far corner of the VIP room, Marcus could see a large cake sitting on a table covered with a pink cloth with gold trimmings. In that same room was a temporary fixture of a stripper's pole with neon lights illuminating from the walls directing light towards it. There were three ladies sitting on one of the couches that surrounded the pole. Marcus did not recognize the ladies who were dress in high heel shoes, tight dresses and long nails. One lady had a different color for each nail on her fingers, which became conspicuous when she used it to stroke the long jet black weave that hanged gently passed her shoulders. The ladies were too busy preoccupied with themselves to even notice him. There was also two champagne bottles in a large ice bucket on a wooden stand next to them. Crackers and cheese with hors d'oeuvres on a silver tray stood near the stereo system that played music for everyone to hear.

Carter emerged from the restroom, to greet Marcus in the usual way. The two had known poverty as a child growing up; but to see each other together owning their own company and not having to work for someone was unusual to them both. It showed, in how they interacted with each other since the establishment of *Dynasty Records*. At the barber shop they were homeboys, now they are entrepreneur. They are building wealth for themselves, not for someone else. Soon they could, when the time presented itself, sell their shares in the record company and start they own gig.

"Where's Derek," Marcus said as he and Carter walked over to the recording section of the studio.

"He was here earlier, he stepped out," Carter replied sitting down on the corporate leather chair. "Just doing little errands, I guess."

"Who are the ladies out there?"

"I don't know, they were here when I got here," Carter rubbed his chin. "To tell you the truth, Derek invited them here."

"Who, for us?" Marcus grinned.

"Must be."

"The one with the big tits, damn," Marcus laughed as he looked to see if they heard him. "Sista got it going on, for real."

"Derek needs to get here so we can get this party started," Carter said leaning back in his chair. "I haven't busted a nut in a while, man."

"Well you won't have to worry about that," Marcus leaned over to his friend. "When we start making money, you won't have to go to them, they'll be begging for your attention. Women are attracted to money, with money they get security. See how they're over there enjoying themselves, if we didn't have two nickels to rub together, we'd be just a fly on the wall."

The two poured themselves a glass of wine that was sitting on the table next to the mixer.

"So, who's your barber now?" Carter asked.

"I have some guy come to my place," Marcus said.

"To your place?" Carter laughed. "You mean the projects."

"Yeah, I can't believe I'm still there, seeing niggas selling crack all day."

"Well, I guess more money will be coming in soon."

"Yeah, I know," Marcus sighed.

"I can't believe we got this far, even though we had to get the money the way we got it."

"Let's not think about that right now, that's in the past," Marcus looked over at Carter with a stern glance. "Empires aren't built on being timid."

A noise can be heard from outside. The door opened and two men walked down the stairs. Derek was dressed in a suit, underneath a cashmere dark grey trench coat, that almost touched the ground. He sported a black designer leather shoes that looked like the one's politicians wore. Following him down the staircase was Joe-Joe. Joe-Joe looked more casual as he sported his new leather jacket with fir trimmings on the hood. A thick gold chain was seen around his neck.

"We did it!" Derek exclaimed. "We did it; we sold about 18,000 units in the first fucking week!"

"Congratulations Joe-Joe," Carter ran over to Joe-Joe and threw a huge bear hug around Joe-Joe who stood quietly still absorbing his new found fame.

"We've made it to the top ten Rap single on the Billboard chart as of yesterday," Derek continued as he walks over to pour himself a glass of wine. "Cheers, brothers, to our success." The men rubbed their glasses together. "By the end of next week, we should have sold about 120,000 copies. By then the checks should start coming in from our distributor." Derek turned to his friend, "I know Marcus you're dying to get out of the shit hole of yours. Marcus you still sleep on that damn couch?"

Everyone laughed. Carter laughed so hard, he almost fell off his chair.

"We'll be making more money than those damn crack dealers," Derek continued as he paced the floor holding a glass of wine.

"You know I wanted to talk to you about the drug dealers at Marcy and who controls that shit," Marcus interrupted.

"Not now man, we can discuss that another time, right now we're celebrating," Derek took another sip of the wine. "The ladies back there?" he pointed to the VIP room.

"Hell's yeah," Carter confirmed.

"Joe-Joe, maybe it's time for you to leave," Derek chuckled.

"Joe-Joe's getting a lot of attention, I can image," Marcus said.

"He's going to have to moving out of Marcy soon," Derek stated. "The more famous he gets the less safe it is."

Carter nodded his head.

"Too much attention is no good," Marcus said.

"I've been getting a lot of attention lately," Joe-Joe said as he displayed a very nervous look on his face. "I try not to go out much as I used to. I stay in the apartment more; you know what I'm saying?"

"What type of attention?" Marcus asked, looking

concerned.

"Just niggas asking for money, or want me to be a part of this or that. Shit like that, you know," Joe-Joe said.

"Marcus, we gotta keep Joe-Joe safe, he our cash flow," Derek said grabbing Joe-Joe by the shoulders. "Joe-Joe, you and your mother have to find somewhere else to live, now that you're becoming famous. I'd advise you to stay low and under the radar for the time being." Derek started taking off his coat. "Actually, we all got to start doing thing differently. They recently did an article about our label in the Daily News, and our names and pictures are in it. So word is getting out and fast. Pretty soon people will start asking y'all for money."

"I haven't seen the article yet, I hardly read the papers anymore," Marcus said.

"Me too," Carter said. "I'm going to have to find that article."

"You probably won't," Derek said facing Carter. "Words get around fast, I'm sure someone will show you that article. I'm sure by tonight; most of the niggas in the hood will know you. People will start to act different around y'all, like they just met you, an' shit."

"Real talk," Carter mumbled.

"Anyway, let's meet them ladies," Derek said excitedly as he danced to the VIP room.

CHAPTER TWELVE

It's been a while since Marcus last met his daughter. He'd received a quick phone call from her, of all places, from her mother's apartment. Keisha appeared happy and express joy in being able to see her father again. Marcus couldn't wait to see her either. Her birthday was two weeks away and he wanted to plan for them to spend more quality time together. It was the weekend, he had decided today would be a great day to see her. He hadn't left the house, since he last met with the other members of the record label the other day. It had snowed the night before, and people were about cleaning the snow off their windshield. It was only a thin layer, but enough to keep Marcy desolate for an early afternoon, while he sneaked out to meet Keisha.

Marcus spotted his daughter up ahead on the corner of Myrtle Avenue and Throop Avenue. She was wearing a fine leather coat with fur trimmings on the edge of the hood. She had brand new leather boots and a skin tight dark gray jean which displayed her physical maturity. Her gait was quick and lively with an occasional skip. She displayed an innocence that was not visible the last time they met near her school. It was the first time he seen his daughter with a perm. It made her look at little older than she did last time. When she stood in front of her father she didn't have the same look of contempt and discord that preceded her conversations.

"Hello, daddy," Keisha said throwing her arms around her

father.

"Daddy?" Marcus asked jokingly. "You never called me that before. What's the difference now?"

"Nothing, just happy to see you, that's all."

"I see mom's spoiling you."

"No, she didn't," Keisha laughed. "She actually was asking about you," Keisha said. "She wants to know how come you never called her."

"Why would I call her?" Marcus asked. "She's getting money now, right?"

"Yeah, I know," Keisha quickly recalled her encounter with her neighbor. "The girl downstairs showed us an article in the news with your picture in it. You a producer now?"

"Something like that."

"We heard the song that the article was talking about."

"Yeah, I'm working for a company that produced that song you heard. The rapper who sings it lives at Marcy too, matter of fact," Marcus tried to sound as modest as he could.

"Can I meet him, please daddy please," Keisha said excitedly. "He looks so cute."

"Soon enough," Marcus said. "We still trying to adjust to all of this right now, you know."

"Can you come back home with me, dad," Keisha look at her father with admiration.

"Home?" Marcus asked. "With that nigga there with your mom, please."

"No, he's not there anymore."

"What the hell you mean?"

"They broke up," Keisha tilted her head.

"Why?"

"I don't know," Keisha said. "Mom wants to see you."

Marcus was surprised at the suggestion that his daughter made to him. After all these years of fighting him in court and trying to get him to not see his daughter and all of a sudden, in these past days, Thelma wanted to see him. Marcus was torn between anger and lust. Thelma was still in her early thirties, and still had the body to show and prove. Her face was one of her best features, he content. She had a natural beauty about her that didn't require her to wear heavy make-up. That's what attracted him to her in the first place. The last time they met at the court house she had on her tight dress and sandals that was irresistible for him even though they weren't seeing each other again. Marcus thought about what Derek had said a few days earlier, about how people will change when you become successful. Marcus felt bitter that she was only interested in seeing him because of his growing success, not because of the man he was inside. He still had feelings for Thelma, but resented what she put him through.

"Hmm," Marcus mumbled while stroking his chin.

"So what are you a messenger now?"

Keisha grinned.

Marcus wanted to tell her no; but this would be the golden opportunity to let her mother see what she had lost.

"I'll be there tonight!" Marcus said abruptly. "You tell her that!"

Knock! Knock!

Marcus waited patiently by the front door of the apartment. A young lady opened the door. She was partly dress; her short nightly robe revealed her smooth caramel skin. Marcus could only guess what she had underneath. The temperament of Thelma was very different from their last encounter. She was open, soft, and sentimental. Her femininity was displayed in the way she smiled this time as well as her body language which exhibited submission.

"Hi," she said. "Aren't you kinda late?"

"I don't know, am I?" Marcus said looking kind of puzzled.

"Just kidding," she showed an even bigger smile. "Come on in."

Thelma still had that cute face that he remembered. Her dimples always got the best of him; they were irresistible, but this time he had to stay strong. This woman could not be trusted, he thought. He knew what she wanted, and he knew what he wanted from her. It wasn't an even exchange. She wanted another child. Keisha would be twenty in a couple of years, which would suspend Thelma's income. Seeing Thelma in her short evening robe reminded him of the good ole days of stopping by and having her ride him on the bed. She was very aggressive; she knew how to work her hips to the rhythm of the music that was playing on the small boom box that she kept near the bed. This time he brought a condom just in case.

"Can I get you something to drink?" she said leading him to the living room where the sofa was.

"Soda would be nice," Marcus replied.

"Soda with what?" she asked.

"Nothing, just soda."

Thelma left the room, and later walked in with daughter who greeted her father briefly, and left to her room for the night. It was probably the first time the three had been together in the same place.

"I see you now a big time producer and all," Thelma said. "I'm surprise you still up there in the hood."

"Not yet," Marcus drinking a cold can of orange soda. "We only produce one single so far." Marcus leaned back on the old sofa and placing his new Jordans on the wooden stand in front of the sofa. "We're now working on a full album. It should be done in a couple of days."

"But you made money from that song right?" Thelma said

suddenly.

"Yeah, we did," Marcus replied. "But we still have a long way to go. The distributor takes a cut, a large one too…then there's the owner of the label, and the technician who mixes the tape. Everybody has to get paid including the artist. By the time it gets to me there's little or nothing left."

"So where did you get the money from to start a record company?" Thelma inquired. "I mean, the article in the paper says you are one of the owner of…I believe it's called *Dynasty* or something?"

Marcus knew he had to be careful with his words, he could sense a little suspicion in Thelma's voice which started to trouble him. "Well, he's a friend of mines, he started the company, you know, I work for him basically, you know."

"Yeah, I understand…isn't he the president."

"Right."

"But the paper says you own part of the company."

"I understand what the paper says…but I'm actually an owner in the sense that I help produce the records, you know?" Marcus became uncomfortable. He had hope that their conversation would never have come to this topic, but it was too late, Thelma wouldn't leave it alone. "I told you…I'm not really an owner."

"How did this Derek guy get the money to start it?" Thelma said gazing at him.

"How the fuck do I know!" Marcus exclaimed. "Do we need to keep talking about this shit?" Marcus finished his drink. "By the way, why are we talking about how much money I'm getting, aren't you getting child support?"

"I'm not talking about money; I was just hoping we could get back together. Besides, I could use a new refrigerator, and a new TV set. You went off to prison and shit, and left me with Keisha," Thelma got up on her feet after sensing that

Marcus wanted to leave. "What was I supposed to do, I needed money, and I still do. Last I fucking remembered when we first met; all you ever talked about was starting a family and shit, buy your own house. What about the American dream you talked about back then, huh?"

"What about the nigga you dating?" Marcus asked.

"What nigga?" Thelma shouted. "I ain't dating him no more, can't you see?"

Marcus remained silent. It was the best he could do with an angry woman in his mist.

"So, are we getting back together or what?"

"Why didn't you ask me this before...you know the last time I was here, when you throw me out of your place," Marcus glared at Thelma. "What was different about me then?"

"You barged in," Thelma said. "Besides, I was with somebody back then."

"Well, just in case you didn't know, I'm still the same person that I was back then."

"No you aren't," Thelma said moving closer to him soft eyes. "Back then, you were a broke ass nigga with no future."

Marcus closed his eye momentarily, just long enough that his former girlfriend didn't take note of it, and wondered what his next step should be. He searched for answers from within. She wanted him back, but for all the wrong reasons, he thought. She was a girl that he grown to love over the first years they were going out. Her love was like a light switch that could be turn on and off at convenient times. She wasn't interested in making the hard decisions that would build a foundation for her to break the cycle of her mother and leave the projects. She just turned to every feel good situation that came about in her life.

"You're independent now," she stated.

"What about when I was trying to be independent, hustling on the street trying to make a few bucks."

Thelma remained silent with her arms folded in front of her chest.

"It was only when I was buying you shit, and taking you to mad parties, that's when I was getting your attention. The moment my hustle broke down, and I wasn't able to feed your selfish appetite, that's when you started talking to other niggas."

"Hmm, wasn't you the one who stop coming around," Thelma cried irritably.

"No, I had made my decision to let you be, and moving on with my life," Marcus answered. "That when you ended up pregnant. Looks like you didn't want to let me go."

"Keisha was an accident," Thelma uttered.

"Was she?" Marcus said sardonically turning his head to look at Thelma sitting next to him on the large sofa.

"Why you say it like that."

"Just asking, that's all."

Marcus was surprise to see that it was Thelma who was the one who appeared to be pleading with him to take her back. It was he who had to jump through hoops and crawl through wires to beseech her attention. It appears that she may have noticed that he may have more options, because of his new found fame; options that weren't there during the cold and enduring days he spent going out with her. The questions that remain in his mind were whether or not to trust her, to keep her, or to move on with someone else. Thelma was raised in the very same housing project with her mother who died from lung cancer.

"It's getting kinda late, I best get going," Marcus stood up from the sofa. As he walked to the end of the living room, Thelma approaches him and grabs his left arm. "I don't know what to think, Thelma, I really don't."

"There's nothing to think about," she said, gazing in his eyes, as the two stood looking at each other, wondering what the next step would be. "So you just gone leave me like that."

Marcus found himself sitting back on the couch. He knew what she was doing. She knew his weaknesses; she knew his passions, and his cravings. It gets him every time. There was no way out, once he saw her cherry lips. He could feel his heart racing and the drop of sweat that rolled from his brow down his chest. He was hoping she wouldn't notice his erratic breathing as he tried to talk. To prevent her from noticing his breathing, he sustained from talking. He didn't want her to know how much power she had over him. His fist was tight-clenched and his blood was drumming in his temples, and his eyes darted back and forth from her small breasts down to her panties. It became a constant recycling that drifted him into a partial hypnotic trance. He woke up from it to find himself slouching on the couch with Thelma unrobed kneeling before him. She noticed the bulge in his pants that wanted to be free. Before he could blink his eyes a few times, Thelma already had his penis in her mouth, stroking it with both hands. Moments later, he could hear himself whispering to her as he grabbed the back of her head, "Don't stop...please." She stroked and stroked until he went into a convulsion of ecstasy. Marcus had already made up his mind that it wouldn't be a while before they would meet again. He hoped that this moment would be a turning point in their relationship going forward.

CHAPTER THIRTEEN

Joe-Joe opened his notebook and began rapping, the bass was intense, and it rocked him back and forth as the lyrics flowed from his lips. It was his third song from his album. Joe-Joe had spent the past few days conjuring up the perfect words that would mesmerize a listening audience.

"Great work, man," the technician said to Joe-Joe who walked out of the recording booth with all smiles. "I think we'll go with the one before, I mean they sound the same, but…"

"Yeah, let do that then," Joe-Joe said. "Which ever you think is best."

The technician turned off the mixer and got up from his chair. "Alright we'll go with that, I guess that'll be all for tonight; I'll lock up."

Joe-Joe left the studio, and walked up Broadway and saw a gypsy cab letting an elderly couple off. Joe-Joe ran just in time and hollered at the cab that stopped to pick him up. It was just past sundown and quite cold and windy as the car sped down the road. Joe-Joe was upset that the driver left one of the windows half opened, letting the cold breeze from outside blow in his face. Joe-Joe didn't wear a scarf and his neck was exposed to the wind rushing from the open window as the car dashed up Broadway. It was only a half a mile left anyway, he thought, he would just bear the pain. Joe-Joe signaled the driver, who pulled up alongside the curb to let him out. It was a quick walk from Broadway to the Marcy projects. He got off at Myrtle Avenue and walked towards Marcy Avenue.

Joe-Joe pulled his hood over his head and kept his hands in his coat pockets to protect them from the frigidity of the cold, and placed his notebook under his arm. He walked with his chin down to block the breeze from touching his neck. As he approached the housing complex he noticed that there were a few people who didn't seem to be bothered by the cold temperature since they didn't seem to be traveling anywhere in particular but merely loitering around the sidewalk and waiting by the telephone booths that stood on the corners of the streets. A gray Honda Accord pulled up out of nowhere, stop at the corner where a young man with a dark blue baseball cap was standing. The man in the car handed the young man a few bills, they shook hands and the car sped off down Marcy Avenue almost hitting Joe-Joe as he crossed the street.

As Joe-Joe walked along the avenue, he saw a young lady in her thirties sitting on the floor near the playground on Myrtle and Marcy Avenues, smoking a glass pipe while holding a lighter to the bottom of it. Her breasts were exposed through her unbutton coat, and the cold air didn't seem to faze her. She placed her complete and undivided attention towards the substance she was inhaling through her mouth. He couldn't help but noticed her partially opened legs shaking as the feeling of ecstasy engulfed her as white smoke oozed out of her mouth. She placed the lighter to the glass pipe a second time, inhaled and seconds later exhaled a cloud of smoke while her eyes caught Joe-Joe staring at her. Joe-Joe felt a flash of anxiety overcome him and he continued to walk down Marcy Avenue.

Joe-Joe tried to remain unnoticeable amongst the few young men that loitered near the front entrance of his building. As he walked to the main door of the building, he could see a young man in a leather goose bomber jacket and a ski cap walking up behind him. Joe-Joe reached into his pocket to retrieve his keys which was buried in his front pocket along with a few loose change and a gold chain he removed after getting out of the cab. Before he could pull his keys from his pocket a voice could be heard from behind him.

"Joe-Joe?" the voice said. "Is that you my nigga."

Joe-Joe turned around to see an old friend from the block. It was Devon. He had spoken with a different tone of voice. Devon was dress in his usual attire, black leather goose-down jacket, dark colored baggy jeans and bright yellow pair of timberlands. He was tall with broad shoulders and always had a droopy looking face, as if he hadn't slept in weeks. His eyes possessed a vacant stare that was visible when making eye contact.

"Hey, what's up," Joe-Joe said. "It's been a while."

"What you been up to?"

"Nut'in much."

As Joe-Joe and Devon talked, another man could be seen receiving money from someone who parked along the side of the road, only to drive off down towards Flushing Avenue.

"I see you're too big to talk to anybody anymore," Devon said.

"Nah, I've just been busy writing lyrics, you know."

"Yo, Craig this is Joe-Joe," Devon said to the other man who was placing a series of folded bills in his pocket. "You know the conscious rapper dude." Devon turned back to Joe-Joe and spoke again. "So you making 'dem dead presidents, uh?" Devon said glaring at Joe-Joe who was still separating his keys from the other content in his pocket. "Joe-Joe, here, is too big to talk to us anymore. I guess soon you'll be leaving us without saying good bye?"

"It ain't like that," Joe-Joe said to Devon as he reacted to the cold breeze blowing against his neck. "We all looking to get outta here right?"

"You used to roll with us, but now…"

"Yeah, nigga thinks he's the shit now," said Craig who moved around to stay warm. He was wearing a white sheep skin coat and a matching hat. "I guess he doesn't need to be a runner for us anymore since he's makin' that cash flow."

"Instead of you guys talking shit about me wanting to leave this fucking place, why don't you take the crack money you make and move and get the fuck out of Marcy?" Joe-Joe said flatly staring deeply at the man closest to him. "You know the real reason ya ass still here, it's because you're afraid to leave. You niggas are afraid of the real world."

"Fuck you muthafucka!" Devon exclaimed. "Nigga, I can leave whenever I fuckin' want to. I'm making mad money bitch!"

"Somebody gave me an opportunity and I'm using it," Joe-Joe said. "And besides, I'm making my own money and it's legit."

"Fuck him, he think he betta' then us," Craig said, his eyes glistened as he spoke.

Joe-Joe tried to remain calm, thinking how not to escalate the situation any further. He tried to brace the cold wind tearing at his face, while trying to look tough.

"Yo, Mike, come here," Devon yelled to someone across the street. "This nigga here is now a big time rappa, and think he don't belong here with us losers."

"So you just gon' leave us like that," Craig said to Joe-Joe ominously, reaching for a cigarette. "That's how it's gon' be."

"Fuck that pussy ass nigga," Devon said coldly while stepping back slowly. "It's all good…it's all good, though."

Joe-Joe finally found the key, turns the latch, and opens the door. Joe-Joe sighed as he let the door close behind him, leaving the two men staring at him as he walked to his apartment door.

"Joe-Joe the conscious rappa," was the last thing he could hear one of them saying while laughing through the main lobby door.

Joe-Joe went inside his apartment and passed his mother who was yapping on the phone talking to a friend. He was hardly noticed as he passed by the kitchen and headed to his bedroom. Joe-Joe became frustrated. He was pressured by Derek and Marcus to finish the album and by people within the housing project who were becoming increasingly jealous and envious of his growing success. He began finishing up the last verse on his fourth track called '*What's popping*'.

While lying on his bed, conjuring up rhymes, Joe-Joe began to think about growing up at Marcy and not having a father to guide him through the rough times. Most teens, at Marcy, never met their father and only learned manhood growing up the hard way on the streets. For young black youths, like himself, the mean streets, and their interactions with other people, were the only father they had. Joe-Joe learned to survive by going with the flow. He dropped out of school due to peer pressure from his former classmates who also lived at Marcy. It was not customary for a young black male, living in the hood, to graduate from high school. At Marcy, graduating from high school was essentially going against the norm; a norm that eventually became a culture at the housing project. Going against this norm, meant having to face the backlash of being different. This phenomenon left two career choices; either a career as a drug dealer or a life as a convict, where free food and shelter was provided. This was an abyss that the majority of black males failed to escape. However, there is a third choice that was created by the minority of those who seek to look beyond the veil for a destiny that is different from that of the complacent masses. This third choice was to become a musician or athlete. This choice required more effort than the other two, but few were able to achieve it. These thoughts, which gripped the very core of his being, lead him to the theme of his fifth song on the album. He would call it 'Escape from Marcy'.

After a good fifteen minutes more of brain storming and seeking inspiration for the lyrics to his fifth track, Joe-Joe looked out of his bedroom window for inspiration on how to approach the lyrical content. He saw nothing but decadence and despair, however when he peeped through the curtains.

The crack epidemic had seemed to have gotten worse over the years. Heroin had left the scene only to be replaced by a more ruthless drug, which is far cheaper and more potent. Joe-Joe watched as residence lined up along the sidewalk to buy their ticket out of their desolation; a ticket that lasted for twenty minutes tops. He would see the same residences line up again a few hours later for another ride.

The scene reminded him of the time when he, his mother and his older brother went to Coney Island and waited in line to buy tickets for a rollercoaster ride, only to rush back a few minutes later to wait in line again for another ride. Joe-Joe came to a realization that he never seen before. This realization answered a question that was haunting him for some while now. The answer made him become conscious of the fact that his fifth track, 'Escape from Marcy' had two connotations; it was ambiguous. There was a double meaning in the meaning of the word *escape*, in the title, that he had to express in his song. He would also make 'Escape From Marcy' the title, as well as the overall theme of his debut album.

Joe-Joe open his notebook and started to write down a few verses in his book about the endless cycle of residence going to and from the street corner of the block in the dead of night searching for a way out of their endless pain and misery fueled by poverty and economic racism. He then wrote another two verses describing how the crack epidemic was started by the government to subside the black working class communities into perpetual poverty. He stayed up late pass midnight writing verse after verse after verse, expressing the condition of a community that had no voice and no power. He would be that voice, he would be that power, he thought to himself. He would do what no politician or community leader could ever do. His voice would be a weapon that would fight back against the powers that be.

He wrote about the prison industrial system and how so many potential great minds were wasted being locked up in cages. He wrote a verse about booby traps that were designed to catch less shrewd minded young black men and perpetually keep them in the criminal justice system.

The lyrics were finally finished!

He pushed the curtain aside and stared out the window, and looked up and down Marcy Avenue, past the ghostly lamps that shed a yellowish image upon the neighborhood streets. He saw different faces this time; one of which was Devon, the man he met earlier in front of the building.

Devon was a 'ticket holder', waiting by an unlit section on Marcy Avenue, as residents walk up to him only to hand him money and leave seconds later with their hands in their pockets and their head facing downward. He witness a lady wearing an old coat lying lifeless on the cold concrete floor as others walked over her, some even tripped over her, to get to Devon.

One particular man, who looked frail, could barely walk, limping and staggering as he tried to catch his balance. Joe-Joe sighed dismally as he noticed the man falling towards the ground on the sidewalk; he slowly gets back up on his feet and falls moments later. After the second fall, he crawls on his hands and knees, surging forward towards Devon who patiently waited swinging his arms back and forth with a smile on his face as he turns his head frequently looking to each end of the block.

Joe-Joe rubbed his tearful eyes, as the need for sleep began to creep in. He wanted to leave the window, but he knew the man that was crawling on the concrete floor, on all fours, like a dog. It was Mr. Edwards, who lived two doors down from him. Mr. Edwards slowly crept his way through the cold and blistering wind ever moving closer and closer to the '*man selling tickets*' who refused to meet Mr. Edwards half way. At one point, Joe-Joe almost ran for a knife in the kitchen when he saw Devon taking a series of steps, moving further and further away, only to have Mr. Edwards walk a longer distance to meet him, while an evil smirk could be seen on his face as he continued to swing his arms back and forth looking in both directions.

Mr. Edwards was a man in his early fifties who lost his job working as a front desk security guard. After that experience, Mr. Edwards moved in with his mother who later died shortly thereafter. He never was the same after that dreadful experience. Like many residences at Marcy, Mr. Edwards was never able to recover from his misfortunes; he ended up turning to crack to escape from Marcy.

Joe-Joe squint his eyes as he saw Mr. Edwards digging into his right side pants pocket and pulled out a bill and nervously handed it to Devon who in return threw a small package of crack cocaine on the floor.

Joe-Joe left the window, closed his notebook, cursed the neighborhood under his breath, crawled into his bed and fell asleep with tears in his eyes.

137

CHAPTER FOURTEEN

Marcus received a phone call from Derek, that evening, he wanted to meet up and discuss the production of Joe-Joe's new album. He wanted to meet at the Williamsburg Bridge again, the place where it all happened. He wanted to meet around 8:30pm.

When Marcus left the apartment it was clear and cold, with a sharp, freezing wind sweeping in over Broadway, as he head west. He felt the cold wind rushing across his face like a freight train. His overcoat was turned up about his chin and his hat was pulled low over his eyes. He clenched his fist often to increase circulation from the cold air that was biting it. He had no idea how cold it was prior to leaving his apartment. It was too late to turn around to get his gloves, and perhaps a scarf. He continued to walk forward to Marcy Avenue past the post office where he saw a man selling cassettes. His curiosity got the best of him. As he gazed over the inventory of tapes the man was selling; he noticed two counterfeit copies of Joe-Joe's single 'No Way Out', which he stared at. The old merchant stood with his little table in front of him, shivering in the cold, with a heavy coat that made his sojourn bearable. The coat looked worn and torn from constant wearing. His hair was gray, and his boots looked like they'd seen combat. Marcus knew he was looking at a man that had been beating by the system; thrown to and fro, not completely buried, yet gasping for air.

"I sold four copies of 'dem Joe-Joe's already today," the man said smiling, noticing that Marcus was piercing at them. "He's supposed to be some conscious rappa or some shit like that I suppose."

"Oh, yeah," Marcus said glimpsing him with a cold eye.

"Yes," the old man said, as he moved about to keep warm. "Those go quick, there my best sell."

"How much for the cassettes?" Marcus asked, not knowing whether to feel distain for the man bootlegging his production or to feel pity. Analyzing the cassettes, Marcus couldn't help but noticed the archaic manner in which the cassettes were prepared. They were obviously dubbed using a double cassette boom box player. The illegible scribbling on the side of the jacket case displayed the poor marketability and amateurism of the peddler.

"They're six a piece, but I'll give you one for five, my brotha," the old man said as he paced nervously with his eyes full of anxiety. "Just trying to ma'ka honest living, ya know...it kinda rough out here, man. Sometimes I move about, one day I'm here, the next day I'm in Harlem, Queens, you name it. I gotta go where the money is, ya hear meh."

Marcus grinned. "I hear ya," he said. "How you making out?"

The man shook his head and gazed at Marcus who quickly turned to look over at the direction of the bridge. "Man," the old man said. "Ever since I was a child, I've been hustling like a sharecropper on a Virginia plantation. I can't tell you my life story, but I can tell ya that it ain't easy when ya ass is poor. You don't have a voice or resources to fight the system when it starts fuckin' you like a fat bitch in a dark alley. I was sent to jail when I was seventeen year old because a white racist cop lied on me and planted heroin in my jacket all because I had reported a cop for punching me during a search. After I left jail, man, I couldn't vote, I couldn't get a fucking job, I couldn't get a fucking loan at a bank…the only thing close to working was a part-time job I had handing out flyers and free mini bean pies at a mall on 125th Street in Harlem. I moved in with my sister for a while, and started doing a little hustling here and there, had some projects that I worked on, ya know, selling all kinda shit. I did some drugs too and got hooked and all…"

Marcus reached into his wallet, as the man continued to ramble, and searched for a five, but found five singles waiting in the front, instead. Marcus handed the man the five singles, turned as he started walking away. "It was nice meeting you, my brotha, but I have an appointment with destiny."

"Hey, bro," the old man said. "Aren't you forgettin' some'in?"

"Nah," Marcus turned around while walking backwards. "I have a copy already, take care."

"You too, my brotha, stay strong."

When Marcus had gotten further away from the old man and into the streets heading towards the bridge, he could scarcely restrain tears as it forced its way out of his eyes. The old man left a grave impression on him.

Marcus continued to walk until the bridge became more visible. It was just a short distance ahead, and he could see the commuters walking eagerly adjusting their scarves to escape the relentless cold.

As Marcus got to the entrance of the bridge, he scanned the area for his friend. Just like last time, Derek stood at the same spot, smoking a cigarette looking at the Manhattan skyline and the ships that sailed below.

"What took you," Derek said casually, still looking ahead, as Marcus approached.

"I was talking to this guy," Marcus said. "Would you believe that nigga was selling our hit song?"

140

"Bootlegging?" Derek asked.

"Yeah, but it's all good, though."

There was a deafening silence when the two didn't speak for a few minutes. They both stared at the Empire State Building and the Twin Towers that overlooked the East River.

"No it's not all good," Derek turned to his friend. "No one gets rich picking the crumbs that falls from someone else's success. We did all the work, risking our lives to get that money. We did the hard work producing that song, we did the hard work negotiating with the distributors, and we're doing the hard work so one day we won't have to do the hard work!" Derek took his last puff and threw his cigarette over the side of the bridge. "The man selling our bootleg cassette is a failure. He sits out in the cold day after day, scraping by just to get a hot plate on his lap. He is a fucking failure."

"Yeah, Derek, com' on man," Marcus said expressing anger in his voice. "I mean what about the system...you know how it is."

"I know exactly how it is mutherfucka!" Derek exclaimed. "He's going to stay right where he is before some cop picks him up or should I say the system, picks him up and puts him in jail, if he's lucky."

Marcus nodded his head not because he agreed with Derek, but because he wanted to move the conversation along without any confrontation.

"Do you know the man I'm talking about?" Marcus asked.

"Yes," Derek replied back. "I saw him when I past the post office on my way here. I glimpsed the shit he had on his little table. I see niggas like him all the time in the hood."

"Okay," Marcus said sternly.

"Do you know what happens to niggas like him," Derek continued. "They end up spending their last days in prison when it's too cold for them to stand out there anymore and the booze don't keep him warm anymore."

"So what's your point?" Marcus asked.

"My point is," Derek whispered. "A couple of months ago, we were a nigga like him looking for a future, hustling for a dime, but what did we do...we didn't give up."

"I don't get you," Marcus said putting his hands in his pockets.

"You see, Marcus," Derek moved closer to his friend who seemed bewildered. "He had no passion. Most people don't succeed in life because they lack passion. The same passion that you have when you're desperately seeking to fuck some pretty bitch with a fat ass and a tattoo on her lower back is the same passion you need in order to succeed in this competitive society of ours."

Marcus crossed his arms and resented what he was hearing. It reminded him of days in which he struggled with preserving his manhood; the days when money was nowhere to be found and his future was a dark tunnel with no light at the end.

"Marcus," Derek said gazing at his friend. "There are many projects people undertake every day, but it fails, because it..."

"Because of what?" Marcus interrupted infuriately.

"Because they lack the passion," Derek said tenderly and plaintively. "The man had many projects that came and went in his life, but he didn't maintain the passion for them like we did. He didn't create an opportunity like we did, when none existed."

Marcus tucked his hands in his pants pocket again and looked over at a couple walking from the Manhattan side of the bridge that timidly kept looking back and forth at them as they walked by.

"Look ahead," Derek said pointing to lower Manhattan.

"What do you see?"

"The Twin Towers...the Brooklyn Bridge...Manhattan."

"Do you know what built it?" Derek asked.

"Money?"

"No," Derek said infuriatingly. "Passion, not money, nigga. You see those niggas you be seeing at Marcy selling that shit all day all night with wife beaters and du-rags on, they got money, but I don't see them building shit with it. Black people got money, but no passion. That great city you see in front of you was built on passion!"

Without responding, Marcus remembered for a split second how his mother used to tell him that his father wanted to open a restaurant with some money he won in a lawsuit but would always find excuses for not doing it, until he ended up spending it all on drugs and women.

"Look, Marcus," Derek said trying to get his friend's attention. "The last time we were here together on this bridge, you and I had nothing, not even two nickels to rub together. But, we could have complained how the system this or that to us...right? But no, we found a solution, I know we robbed a place and ended up killing two people, but look, we are standing here as two producers with a record label that's about to break out. You see, we could have been like those niggas sitting on the steps and walking around the Brooklyn projects, right? No, we took the resources that we needed and started what may become an empire if we keep our passion. Who knows where this could lead. We can be hip-hop moguls if we maintain that passion."

Marcus tried to understand what Derek was saying. He felt that Derek failed to acknowledge the institutional side to racism that crippled opportunities for blacks in America, as they had talked about on many occasions.

"As I said before," Derek said, getting a little emotional.

"No one is going to give you anything in this world. You have to take it and in some cases, kill for it. That is what we are doing and that is what that man and a lot of those dumb ass niggas failed to do. He failed to maintain the passion...the fire. Passion is what built all the shit you see there, over there." Derek pointed towards Manhattan with his chin. "Joe-Joe wrote the lyrics for 'No Way Out' and produced the beats for the song as well, because he had a passion to produce the song. There are many rappers out there who wrote and compose shit but never got further than a park bench, whether Marcy or otherwise, because the flame didn't stay lit and they gave up the struggle."

"I understand," Marcus said trying to avoid the wind in his face. The wind was blowing more steadily at the bridge; there were no buildings to block it. "So why did you bring me out here in this fucking cold?"

"Did you speak with Joe-Joe, since?" Derek said while rubbing his hands together.

"No, not really."

"Well, he called me this morning to tell me that he completed writing the lyrics for all nine tracks," Derek cleared his throat and continued. "He rapped some of the songs to me over the phone. I must say I was completely unaware how moved I was until I saw smoke coming from the kitchen, the whole fucking kitchen was in smoke. I did not hear the fucking alarm. I forgot that I was cooking eggs and bacon on the stove."

"Damn, that good?" Marcus was in disbelief.

"Yeah, that good!" Derek exclaimed. "He even has the beats for the songs in his head he said, too. We're going to start recording tomorrow night. I called Richie, and he's going to be at the studio to do sampling and mixing as usual. We need to get this shit out to the distributors right away."

"Man I never expected anything like this," Marcus leaned against the gate that run along the sides of the pedestrian walkway. "Never thought he'd finish this quick."

"That reminds me," Derek said contentedly. "I called the distributor and they told me the single 'No Way Out' sold 149,000 copies so far."

"Get the fuck outta of here!"

"Yeah," Derek said. "The checks should be coming in soon. By the way, I even heard niggas bought new Sony Walkmans just so they could listen to it on cassette."

"I like that."

Derek smiled and adjusted his coat to prevent the wind from hitting his neck.

"You know what I was thinking," Marcus said. "Every waking hour of the day them niggas out there selling crack, day in and day out making hundreds of dollars a day, thousands a week, but yet they still poor, where is all that fuckin' money going and to who?"

Derek paused, wiped his face. "Man, you got me there."

"Man that money could be put to good use, like buying real estate."

"Now you're thinking like me."

"I'm serious."

"That's a whole different ballgame," Derek said as he stepped back and couldn't believe where Marcus was going with the conversation.

"Somebody else is getting rich off of us."

"You're starting to sound like me," Derek stood and shook his head. "Producing music is much safer, and besides you don't have to look over your shoulders all the time."

"It was just a thought."

"I hope so," Derek said and looked around at the J train passing over the bridge. "It's too fucking cold out here." The two men started walking towards the Brooklyn entrance of the bridge. "So, I'll see you at the studio tomorrow?"

"Yeah, I'll try to make it," Marcus said.

"You and Joe-Joe can go together, if you like."

"Sound good, take care."

Marcus made his way east on Flushing Avenue, the icy wind pick up again, making the walk unbearable. He thought about whether to buy food on his way home or to see what his mother had prepared. His appetite and the sight of his favorite fried chicken spot made his decision quite simple. It was at the next block. The place was full, but being out most of the night, the wait, for him, was worthwhile. He ordered two pieces of chicken and French fries and an orange soda. He decided to eat it at home; a gypsy cab ride to the projects would bring him home in minutes.

On his ride home, he thought about the idea of finally being able to leave Marcy, once Joe-Joe's album dropped. The public would eat it up like shrimp fried rice. The label would make millions of dollars. His mother would finally have a real home to live in, away from the madness and decadence that plagued Marcy. He already knew what car he would purchase. He had his eyes on a Mercedes that rolled by when he was waiting for the light to change one day.

Once home he tried to avoid the losers pacing the street corners despite the cold. He tucked his head down, and hoped the cold and frigid temperature would keep the undesirables from inquiring about who he was or even recognize him. He was able to slip pass a few young men in hoodies and leather coats on the block where the entrance to his apartment was. Except for a few head turns and raised eyebrows, Marcus was able to enter into the apartment undisturbed. His mother must be asleep, he thought to himself as he opened the apartment door. He swiftly walked to the bathroom to relieve himself from having to wait so long. The rushing sound of his urine hitting against the toilet must have woken his mother up.

"Marcus," he heard his mother say as he headed to the kitchen to remove his food from the bag.

"Yeah, Ma."

"I thought I heard something," his mother rubbing her eyes, as she walked from her bedroom.

"Just fixing something to eat," he said reaching for a fork.

She turned around and headed back to her room, but stopped. "Oh, one other thing, there was two gentlemen here, maybe a little more than thirty minutes ago, asking for you."

"Asking for me!" Marcus exclaimed wondering who that could be. He paused to recall if he made any arrangements with anyone but couldn't.

"Yeah, they said they were from the NYPD," his mother continued. "They said they were detectives, and they said they were hoping you would help them locate some guy name Derek." His mother scratched her head, trying to recall something. "Oh, yes, Derek Sanders, do you know him?" She glazed at her son with a prying look on her face handing him a card with the police officer's information on it. "They said to call them at this number."

Marcus took the card and left it on the kitchen table. Marcus felt like the world had stop moving. That brief moment felt like eternity. He could feel his blood racing through his veins. The sweat burst through the skin of his forehead in tiny beads, and he paused and mopped his dark face with his right hand. He could not hear his mother speaking to him and could only see her lips moving.

"Marcus!" his mother yelled. "Marcus, boy you been drinking?"

"No, I haven't eaten since," he said, attempting to mask

his anxiety. "That's all, Ma?" Marcus pulled the chair out from the table and tried to sit. He waited until she looked away. He didn't want her to see his awkwardness when he sat down or see him expressing any guilt in his behavior. "Did they say what about?"

"No, but I don't know what he want with you," his mother inquired. "Was you involved with anything I should know about?"

"Nah," Marcus said. "Derek is a busy guy, so it could be anything."

"Is that the guy you work for?"

"Yes, Ma."

Marcus had lost his appetite; he could not take a bite of the chicken thigh he held in his hand. His mind was racing back and forth; he felt his life was crashing down all over in front of him like an avalanche. He started to question himself. How did they found out, was there finger prints left behind, was there evidence they forget to removed; what could it be? He felt a sharp pain in his gut jabbing him like a spear sinking deeper and deeper inside of him. He felt out of breathe, yet he wasn't running. He felt weak in the knee, yet he wasn't injured. This was just a passing moment, he reassured himself, maybe they knew Derek was a big time producer, and thought he may have information about something that happened recently. After all, the incident at the check cashing place, happened months ago, if the police had found anything, surely they would have found it already, he thought.

Marcus knew he had to call Derek to tell him the police were looking for him. They must have gone to his old address in the projects.

Since the incident, Derek had moved out of his grandmother's apartment and got something private for himself somewhere in Fort Greene. "How did they know I lived here?" Marcus whispered. Marcus recalled that the article in the Daily News mentioned that he lived at Marcy; and besides they could easily get his address from his prison records, he thought to himself. He would wait until tomorrow morning to talk to Derek and Carter about the police inquiry. He was too restless to talk to anyone now. His heart was still pounding in his chest while cold sweat rolled down his back and dampened his undershirt. A few minutes pasted and he was calm now, and he was able to clear his mind of all the misfortunes that befallen him.

Derek had promised him that the operation would be flawless. He had ironed out everything for the two of them, there were no mistakes, they wore gloves, masks, and everything. "Maybe I'm rushing to conclusion," Marcus said to himself while preparing to go to bed for the night. After hearing what sounded like gunshots coming from outside, he settled in to the large sofa and laid his head to rest.

CHAPTER FIFTEEN

Marcus was awoken by three knocks at the door. He was not used to hearing the door knock at 8:00am in the morning. It must be one of the neighbors, he reckoned, since he had heard a few gunshots last night. He quickly pulled a T-shirt over his head and walked over to the door after a second series of knocks was heard.

"I'm coming!" Marcus cried out as he ran to the door.

When he opened the door, there were two white gentlemen standing in front of it. The one closest to the door was a short man of a heavy set built; he wore an unbuttoned rain coat with a gray suit underneath it. The other man who stood next to him was much taller, but slightly younger and wore sunglasses. Marcus almost fainted. He tried desperately to keep his composure.

Marcus cleared his throat. "Can I help you?" he asked.

"Yes, we're looking for Marcus Carlton," the short man said.

"I'm Marcus," Marcus mumbled. "What do you want?"

"Good morning, Marcus," the short man said firmly as he extended his right hand to Marcus who shook it. "I'm detective Mark Olson and this is detective Robert McMillan; we're from the NYPD homicide unit."

Marcus passed his right hand over his face as he heard his mother leaving the bathroom.

"Marcus," the detective said. "We were here yesterday

but your mother said you weren't home at the time. We're investigating a case, a homicide, a double homicide actually, that took place during the summer at the check cashing center on Nostrand Avenue. I'm not sure you've heard about it on the news or what have you, but we looking for...I believe he is a friend of yours." The detective paused. "Derek Sanders, do you know him?"

"Marcus!" Marcus' mother yelled. "Who's at the door?"

"It's me, ma'am, remember from yesterday?" Detective Olson said waving his hands.

"Oh, hi."

"Just asking your son a few questions, if you don't mind," the detective said.

"Go right ahead," his mother said, standing by the door, out of view, but close enough to overhear the conversation.

The detective looked at Marcus with a cold stare. Marcus could feel his mother staring at him, so much so that it affected his behavior. Marcus' hand began to shiver as a mild amount of sweat accumulated at his brow. He tried desperately to conceal his nervousness and the guilt in his eyes.

"Yeah, I know him," Marcus said uneasily. "What do you want with him?"

"We just wanted to ask Derek a few questions about the incident."

"You think he was involved in it?"

"Not necessarily, but he may be able to provide us with some information regarding our investigation."

"I mean...I can tell him you looking for him...sometimes he passes by, you know."

"Fair enough," Detective Olson said smiling. "I left my business card with your mother...do you still have it?"

"Yes."

"Well it was nice speaking to you Mr. Carlton," the

Detective shook Marcus' hand and he and the other detective turned to leave. "Oh, one other thing, Mr. Carlton," the Detective said touching the top of his head as he and the other detective stood across the hallway near the elevator. "How long have you known Mr. Sanders?"

"Oh, uh, since high school, I guess, but we never talked."

"Where do you work?"

"I work for Derek, as an assistant."

"Where?"

"At his record company in Bushwick."

"What kind of work did you do prior to that?"

"Nothing, I wasn't working then."

"You were unemployed?"

"Yes."

"For how long?"

"Since I left prison."

The detective grinned and nodded his head. "Prison," he repeated. "Have a good day Mr. Carlton, we'll see you soon."

The two men made their way to the elevator before leaving the complex.

Marcus closed the door behind him. Without notice, Marcus' mother jumped in front of him.

"What the hell is going on?" she exclaimed. She stared at her son with a look of despair in her eyes. She could not believe what she heard. "Are you involved in something I should know about, Marcus?"

"No," Marcus replied. "They were just asking questions."

"Questions about you and Derek," his mother demanded. "About the killing!"

"No."

"No, what?"

"Take it easy, you're jumpin' to conclusions."

"No I'm not!"

"Yes, you are."

"In case you didn't know," his mother said pointing her fingers at him and moving closer to him. "People around here have been talking about how you've become famous all of a sudden. Where did Derek get that money from to start that company?"

"He had the money already."

"Nigga, don't lie to me, I ain't stupid...I know that nigga didn't just live in the projects and then started a company like that. People are talking, words get around you know. That's why the cops are scoping him."

Marcus tempted to walk away.

"I didn't say nothing to you, Marcus, because I figured Derek was a high class drug dealer or something, but I figured you needed a job and all, so I stayed out."

"Please...drug dealer," Marcus laughed and then became serious. "Just stay out, and stop getting emotional over nothing."

"I just don't want you to get in trouble, that's all," his mother shouted as she wiped the water that settled in her eyes. "This neighborhood is not a place for anyone to raise a child." She held the back of her head and sat down on the large sofa where her son sleeps. "I watched what happened to your father and your brother and I see the same thing is going to happen to you."

"Naw, everything gon' be alright, Ma."

Marcus rushed to the bathroom to wash up; he brushed his teeth and got dress.

"Where you going," his mother said looking wildly.

"I'm going to work, Ma."

"Good god."

"I'll see you soon."

Marcus threw his coat on and ran out the door. He

checked to see if Joe-Joe was home, but his mother told him Joe-Joe had left already.

It was Saturday morning and people were about Christmas shopping along the avenue. Marcus pushed his way through the crowded streets of Brooklyn, where people went from store to store looking for the best bargains they could find. Christmas was the last thing on Marcus' mind; he was more intent on making sure it wouldn't be his last Christmas as a free man. Occasionally, someone would swing their shopping bag in front of him, expecting him to move out of the way. The incidents made him more agitated as he raced to get to the studio. "Next time watch where ya going," he yelled at a woman who's shopping bags were as big as her stomach. She quickly turned around but didn't know where the voice came from. The streets were chaotic, as last minute shoppers swayed their vehicles away from pedestrians walking in the middle of the street. People were behaving like mindless sheep, acting on impulse from signs that read '*50% off Today Only*', or '*Everything Must Go By New Year's*'.

Marcus made his way to Bushwick Avenue to catch a gypsy cab to Bushwick. One cab pulled up along the curb, with three passengers in it; one in the front and two in the back.

"Are you goin' to pay for two, ma'am," the driver said to the woman in the back seat who had a boom box radio sitting on the available seat next to her.

"Where the fuck am I going to put it," she scream at the driver. "There's no room in here!"

"Are you paying for two," the driver insisted as his voice rose higher. "That's all I'm asking."

"Yes!"

The car moved swiftly into traffic and sped off down Bushwick Avenue leaving Marcus standing with his hands in his pocket. It was a no win situation at this time of the year. Marcus sighed and decided to walk further down the street. Each cab that drove by had the same situation with customers taking up more space with their items.

Anxiety began to creep up on him as he saw a police car with flashing lights heading towards him. He could feel his heart pounding in his chest as he gasp for air. Cold air rushed into his lungs like a jet stream, causing his chest to become numb from the constant intake of arctic air. He could feel blood pulsating at his neck which created an immediate headache that felt like his head was going to explode. The police drove up next to a parked car that had two African American men in the front seat. Guns were drawn from the officer's waist belt, as the two men look up at the officer's pointing guns at them. Marcus was relieved and almost fainted alongside a parking lot across the street where it all took place. He was able to catch himself and changed his gait quickly to mask suspicion from any onlookers. He glimpsed a bodega down the street about a block away, surely a cup of coffee would soothe him for a while until he got to the studio, was his thought.

The warm cup of coffee against his cold lips, and down his throat gave him a calming sensation. Moments later he felt the caffeine kicking into his system. That was what he needed.

After walking about a mile, Marcus finally arrived at the studio. Carter and Richie were sitting at the mixing table in front of the recording booth wearing headphones. A sense of gloom stifled the air in the room which they sat. A dismal look from Carter, who turned to look at him, told him something was wrong. He realized he had walked in the middle of a recording session that was already in progress. Marcus paced the area; Derek was nowhere to be found.

A few moments past and Carter came out of the studio to

greet him. Carter was wearing a wool sweater with dark blue jeans with designer leather boots.

"What's up my nigga," Carter said with a hint of melancholy. "Haven't seen you in a bit."

"I know, I've been here and about."

"I know you must be wondering where Derek is?"

"Yeah."

"He called and said he'll be late."

"Why, what happened?"

"He said he was at the police station last night," Carter sighed and looked to the floor. "It's not looking good for us."

"Did the police come to your house?" Marcus asked.

"Yeah, they did, last night," Carter replied. "They asked me a few questions and left."

"They came to my place this morning and did the same thing."

"I wonder why they took Derek to the station instead, but not us."

"Who knows, I had to walk all the way here, couldn't find a cab if my life depended on it."

"Did you guys leave any evidence in the place?" Carter asked. "Maybe someone seen Derek when he walked in the front door, but then again he was wearing a mask or something like that, right?"

"I don't know, I think so," Marcus felt a depressed feeling passed through him. "I try very hard not to think about that day, really. You don't know, Carter, how much I try to not remember what happened that day. I was able to block it out of my mind."

"I know we never talked about it."

"We have to talk about it now, they going to question us again sooner or later."

"The way I see it," Carter said. "If they had hard evidence

against us they would've arrested us, don't you think?"

"Yeah, I guess, but I can tell you one thing though," Marcus said, his eyes widened. "I'm not going back to jail, no matter what. I did hard times in that place; it's not fun to be locked up with niggas who hate you and a system that's constantly trying to break you, especially if you're black."

The music had stop playing, and the two turned towards the young man coming out of the booth. It was Joe-Joe; he smiled for the first time and waved at Marcus.

"How did you like it," Joe-Joe asked, looking up and brightening visibly.

"Which one was that, I mean which track?" Marcus asked.

"That was '*Body Count*'," Joe-Joe replied. "It has a more gangster touch to it. In it I rap about the shoot outs that be happening at Marcy sometimes and the gang violence and shit. I figured I'd take on the west coast gangster rappers with this one. They said something about me the other day; this is for them. It's track number seven, it's a diss track."

"Shit is tight," Carter said.

"So you basically rap about your experiences at Marcy?" Carter asked.

"Experiences at Marcy, yeah, what I be seeing at night," Joe-Joe agreed. "Marcy is all I know, never lived anywhere else."

"Well it's time for you to escape and get the fuck out!" Marcus exclaimed. "Like all of us in here; the hood is no place for anyone to live. It makes you do shit you don't need to be doing, ya feel me?"

"I feel ya," Joe-Joe said cheerfully.

Joe-Joe maintained his cheerfulness as Marcus looked at him. Deep down Joe-Joe was a little apprehensive of leaving the only place he knew, but he knew it was necessary.

"I know Derek talked about this before, but once the

album drops, you're leaving that place for good," Marcus placed his left hand on Joe-Joe's shoulder. "He mentioned a place close to where he lives now in Fort Greene."

"How about Jamaica, Queens, I have an aunt that lives out there in Cambria Heights," Joe-Joe stated.

"Yeah, that too, wherever you want to live, Joe-Joe, it's your call," Marcus assured him. "But you just can't stay at Marcy anymore."

Joe-Joe nodded.

"How many tracks you recorded so far," Marcus said.

Richie stood up from his seat near the mixer and looked at Marcus. "So far we recorded one track; I was able to sample the beat that Joe-Joe created along with a few trumpet sounds in the background. That was the song you were hearing."

"When did you sample the beat?" Marcus asked.

"Two days ago," Richie answered. "All Joe-Joe needed to do was hum the beat for me over the phone, I did the rest."

"Wow, awesome," Marcus cried, as he grabbed Joe-Joe by the neck with his arm wrapped around it, and kissed him on the back of the head. "You the shit!"

"We might actually be able to get this done by New Year's," Richie said. "We've already started working on the album cover. It will have a picture of Marcy...the building, that is, in the background with Joe-Joe's face, when he was younger, superimposed on it...or we may just put the Williamsburg Bridge on it instead of his picture...who knows, it's Derek's call."

"Sounds good," Carter interjected. "I hope we have a release date."

"Yeah, Derek is working on that," Richie said. "We're trying to push it so we can do a New Year's Eve release party." Richie looked at his watch and turned to look at Joe-Joe. "Ready to record... '*The Passion*'?"

"Hell yeah," Joe-Joe responded delightfully. "Let do this shit."

"Wait," Marcus quickly demanded. "Who came up with this song...the title?"

"Derek wanted me to call it that, when I rapped it for him over the phone the other day," Joe-Joe said. "He had me change the lyrics around a bit...like add some shit he talked about over the phone. I was planning to call it something else, but Derek insisted I call it that. It's what drives us all, he said."

"So, what's it about?" Carter seemed as if he was missing out on something.

Joe-Joe walked to the booth, looked over at Carter and said, "It's about fulfilling your dreams and going after what you want in life, shit like that."

"What track is that," Carter yelled as Joe-Joe was closing the door.

"Number...nine," Joe-Joe yelled back and closed the door.

Everyone walked over to the mixing station and sat down while Richie prepared the recording of the new track. The beat started; it had a slow tempo, with a heavy bass kick to it. It had a kind of jazzy feel to it, and then Joe-Joe's rapping started. It was steady, and it harmonized perfectly to the jazzy beat that was playing in the background. It was almost a cross between R&B and Rap.

Derek walked in and made his way into the studio. He was quite modest in his entrance, and less confident than usual. His eye was blood-shot and his face was rough and unshaven. He appeared drossy like he hadn't slept in years. Marcus was not used to seeing Derek in this manner. It appeared that the recent events had shaken him at his core.

"Merry Christmas," Derek said. "Happy New Year."

"Thanks," said Marcus approaching his friend. "How's it

going?"

Derek held his head down and removed his coat, and remained silent for a moment. "Did you hear what happened to me?"

"Yes," Marcus affirmed. "They came to my place as well. This morning...well actually last night when I was out with you on the bridge."

"Last night, late...late last night they almost broke down my fucking door and told me to get dress and brought me to the station. They questioned me for hours, asking me all these fucking question and shit. Even when I told them that I wanted to see a lawyer they still wouldn't let me go until after four in the morning."

"You look fucked up, man," Marcus said.

"I haven't slept all day."

"I can see."

The two walked over to the back of the studio, leaving Richie and Carter at the mixing station.

"I'll be leaving in a little bit, though," Derek collapsed on the sofa in the VIP area of the studio. I need to get some sleep. I drive home first and came here after eating a little something. I don't know how they got my address; I don't live with my grandma's no more in the hood."

"You're famous know," Marcus chuckled. "There's nowhere to hide." Marcus turned to his friend and realized that he was not paying attention to what he said. "What they say to you, what happened?"

"Listen, man, we got enemies in that fucking place of yours."

"What do you mean?"

"Where you fucking live."

"Marcy?"

"Yeah," Derek turned and looked at him.

Derek opened his eyes and into them Marcus saw an unbridled anger of an half broken man who refused to quit.

Derek started to explain what happened. "When the police was doing their investigation about the place...the Korean place...they went to the projects a few weeks ago where you live and niggas was saying how you and I and Carter all of a sudden get money to start this label we got going here."

"Who said that?" Marcus asked.

"I don't fucking know, but that's what the police was asking me about."

"Where you got the money?"

"Yeah," Derek continued. "That's none of their business; besides I think they know about the jacket I wore."

"Why you say that?"

"They asked me if I ever worked for Con Ed and shit. I said no."

"So what happened then?"

"I kept asking for a lawyer, and they let me go."

"There closing in on us," Marcus said fearfully.

"I know," Derek placed his hand over his face. "Somebody saw me wear the jacket that day but didn't recognize...or didn't see my face; that's where the investigation is heading now."

"We're fucked!"

"Nah, we're not. If we were, they would have moved in and arrested us already. They don't have anything concrete and the investigation will eventually fall short and become cold."

"Hopefully, it stays that way."

"Do me a favor," Derek commanded. "Say nothing to the police. I'll tell Carter to do the same thing."

Derek left the room, greeted Carter with a handshake and whispered something to Richie. He grabbed his coat, placed it over his shoulders and gracefully walked out of the studio.

The recording continued all day into the night with occasional breaks in between. Joe-Joe had all the lyrics to his songs memorized; while other parts of the songs were improvised.

It's been three weeks since Joe-Joe started the recording of his debut album and it have been completed. The master copy had been delivered to the distributor along with photographs to be used for the album cover. The release date was set for the day before New Year's Eve. Derek originally had wanted the release day to be New Year's Eve itself, but the distributor wanted the public to get an extra day to listen to the songs before hearing it at the various clubs, radio stations and parties at which time they would be played. The single 'No Way Out' has been played repeatedly on FM radio stations in anticipation of the release of the album. Derek had planned a release party for Joe-Joe on New Year's Eve in Harlem. The place was actually a night club & bar that had hosted other great musicians in the past, which was used to launch their careers. It was large enough to hold about sixteen hundred people, and cheap enough to host an up and coming artist.

CHAPTER SIXTEEN

It was the day of the release party and the club was packed. Derek, Carter, and Marcus were all dress in their new outfits with money they got from the sale of the single 'No Way Out'. Derek was dress in a new wool suit, dark gray in color, tailor-made, with pin stripes, with a pair of black leather shoes. Marcus wore an off white suit he purchased the night before and a pair of white leather sandals. In addition, he wore a matching black tie. Carter wore a black three piece suit with a tan colored vest with a bow tie and black colored leather shoes.

All three men looked their best for an event that they never dreamt would ever happen. Months earlier they were three men living in the ghetto, now they have the potential to become movers and shakers in the world of hip hop.

The party was nice. It was a black younger crowd mostly from Brooklyn and Manhattan. There were a few whites who showed up, mostly from *The Village Voice*, who wanted to meet the up and coming new artist that everyone was talking about. The crowd became restless as the anticipation of Joe-Joe's arrival became imminent. Cheese and crackers was set aside near the opposite walls of the hall, along with waiters who walked around with champagne glasses on trays. Derek had arranged for Joe-Joe to show up after everyone settled in. He was to make a grand entrance.

The moment had finally arrived and Joe-Joe made his way into the dance hall. He was greeted by Marcus and Carter who escorted him to the stage area at the front of the hall. Moments later the music started; it was the title song of his album. The crowd cheered when the music to '*Escape from Marcy*' started playing over the loud speakers. Marcus and Carter walked Joe-Joe, who was wearing his signature outfit: a dark gray hoodie with dark blue jeans and black leather mountain boots, on to the stage where Derek stood holding a microphone. Derek, who was hosting the event, threw his arms around Joe-Joe who shivered with nervousness and anxiety. Derek signaled for the music to stop, put his left arm around Joe-Joe's shoulders and moved him closer to the edge of the stage.

"Ladies and gentlemen," Derek said trying to speak over the crowd who was getting restless. "As president and CEO of Dynasty Records, it is my honor and privilege to introduce to you the man of the hour; the man who will become the next hip-hop superstar... Joe-Joe!"

Everyone cheered and chanted, "Joe-Joe, Joe-Joe, Joe-Joe..."

"It was only a few months ago," Derek continued as the crowd quiet down. "One of my colleagues, who is standing on the stage to my left, who discovered Joe-Joe at the Marcy housing projects where they both lived in Brooklyn. It was at that moment that Joe-Joe's talent was recognized and brought to my attention. Shortly, thereafter, we signed Joe-Joe to the label and began working on his first single, which you all been hearing on the stations and what not. Now we just released his first debut album, yesterday...*Escape from Marcy*, which by the way, according to our distributors, has already sold out in many record stores on the east coast, believe it or not." There were people taking pictures of the two of them on stage. Derek for the first time in his life felt he was on top of the world and couldn't believe it. "Ladies and gentlemen, I want to say that

Joe-Joe grow up in the hard projects of Bed-Stuy, and always dreamt of leaving and becoming a star. Now he is finally fulfilling his dreams and leaving the projects behind for good. Joe-Joe has proven that no matter your circumstances in life, there is always a way out, even when it seems there is no way out." Derek paused and laughed. "I would like to wish you all a Happy New Year." Derek turned to Joe-Joe. "Everyone I give you Joe-Joe," Derek said giving Joe-Joe the microphone.

When the DJ struck the first few beats of 'Escape from Marcy', the crowd erupted and cheered. Once Joe-Joe began rapping, his nervousness ceased. He paced the stage wearing his hood over his head barely showing his face. The crowd picked up with the beat and urged him on, swaying their arms from side to side over their heads as he continued to mesmerize them with his lyrics.

Joe-Joe ended his performance, by shaking hands with people who were at the front of the stage. Joe-Joe walked to the back area where the others were waiting.

Derek, Carter and Marcus were there with champagne glasses in hand. Everyone got up when Joe-Joe entered the room. A man who looked Puerto Rican pulled out a bottle of champagne from a bucket and popped the cork. He poured everyone a glass, and handed Joe-Joe a glass.

"Cheers to our new rain maker!" the Puerto Rican man said his voice high with excitement. "You made us a lot of money today." The Puerto Rican man raised his glass of champagne towards Joe-Joe and drank it before turning to Derek.

"This is Juan, Joe-Joe," Derek said. "He's one of the owners of this club and a good friend of mine."

"Thank you, Juan" Joe-Joe said. "I really appreciate what you have done."

Marcus rose from his seat and asked for quiet before

turning his attention to Joe-Joe. "On behalf of the label, we would like thank you again for all your effort in completing and recording this album for us. I know it wasn't easy to come up with those bad ass lyrics, but we want to thank you." Marcus beckoned for everyone who was sitting to stand up. "I want to make a toast to our raising star, Joseph Ellis, and may the New Year bring more success to you and your family...cheers." Everyone came together to make a toast with their glasses.

Joe-Joe who was gazing out into space, still trying to come to grips with his new found fame, raised his glass and moved it towards the glasses that were converged together over a night stand. He barely remembered what Marcus had said, but he just knew that his life would be different from this point on.

The group continued to party for a while and the crowd outside waited for the New Year to begin. There was a large television in the dance hall area where the crowd watched the New Year's Eve festivities on the screen.

The countdown was already underway, when Derek asked Joe-Joe to greet the crowd once again after the stroke of midnight. The crowd began chanting the countdown while watching it on the big screen from scenes in Times Square, New York. The DJ began playing *Auld Lang Syne* for the crowd who erupted with cheers and laughter.

"Joe-Joe," Juan said suddenly. "Go out there...and give the crowd what they want."

Joe-Joe peeped over at Derek, who pulled out a cigarette from his jacket, and nodded. He felt a sudden rush of tension engulf him in his entire body. He could hear the crowd chanting in the background. He was scared to go out there a second time. He blinked his eyes and stared out into space. The reality of the room fell from him. He was all alone, by himself for a brief moment in time until he heard a voice calling.

"Joe-Joe!" Derek exclaimed. "This is your chance of a life time, man. Get your ass up there on stage."

The beat came on, and he turned to Derek angrily and said, "I want to do '*What's Popping*' instead."

"Can't you hear the crowd," Juan responded. "They're chanting '*Body Count*'. That's what they want to hear. That's the most requested song from your album in the past twenty-four hours, man. It's not about what you want; it's all about the money. You're going to learn real quick…you want to stay in this business…you better learn."

Joe-Joe stood up, threw this hood over his head, partially covering his face, and walked out of the room and was given a microphone from a young lady who stood by the entrance to the stage.

The crowd erupted in applause and cheers when he walked on stage. He had the crowd's full attention, when he spoke on the microphone. "Happy New Year everybody…happy 1990!" he screamed. The music for his song '*Body Count*' continued to play on the sound system. Amazingly, a few of the audience already knew the lyrics for the song as they sang along with him as he paced the stage alluring the crowd while he displayed his hip hop studio gangster persona. He began to rap a few bars from the song:

> *They tried to escape from realities,*
> *I'm tired of all the fatalities,*
> *And the crack bitches wants to suck cock,*
> *I told you, I can't stop,*
> *Until I kill all the crack dealers on my block,*
> *Yeah, with my nine millimeter Glock.*

Joe-Joe began the third verse, and the crowd cheered in anticipation of what was coming. He moved closer to the edge of the stage and rapped:

> *So niggas want to rap about being from Compton,*
> *Yeah and you should, and that's all good,*
> *You must think I'm from Canarsie,*
> *come out to the hood*
> *an' see my body count,*
> *Yeah, where I'm from, niggas, it's called Marcy.*

It was late, when the party ended. Everyone left and it was an hour before the crack of dawn. Marcus ordered a limousine for Joe-Joe. The limo was to take him to Cambria Heights in Queens where he had rented an apartment.

"It's been a long day," Marcus said turning to his friend.

"Yeah, I can't wait to go to bed," Joe-Joe said smiling at his friend who was still a little drunk from drinking all night.

"How are you enjoying your new place up there in Queens?"

"It aight, just a little quiet, though."

"So, you finally escaped Marcy, huh?"

"I never thought I would make it out of the hood, ya know," Joe-Joe said, clearing his throat. "You won't catch my black ass back there for nothin'."

Marcus laughed and playfully tapped his friend on the shoulders. "They say you can take a nigga out of the hood, but you can't take the hood out of a nigga." Marcus giggled and moved closer to his friend. "There's no reason for you to go back there other than to see your mother…and let her come to you instead if you want to see each other, you hear?"

"I feel ya man," Joe-Joe said nonchalantly.

"Fuck Marcy!" Marcus exclaimed staggering a little to catch his balance. "I'll be leaving there too, in two weeks or so. I got this new place, but it's in Bed-Stuy though…the good part."

"That must be my car," Joe-Joe said as he hugged his friend goodbye. "I just wanted to say, you been like a father to me...thank you again for giving me an opportunity when you saw me out there that day. This is how we black folks gotta be...looking out for each other... know what I'm sayin'."

"I love you, man, stay strong, and don't look back...talk to you soon," Marcus said as he wiped a tear from his eye as Joe-Joe walked to the limo that was parked along the sidewalk.

Joe-Joe awakened late in the afternoon after arriving home from the New Year's Eve party. As he sat in bed, in his new apartment, he thought about what the New Year might have in store for him. With his new fame and recognition, he felt additional weight had been placed on his shoulder to produce. Joe-Joe was actually hoping his album wouldn't do too well; if it did, that would create too much pressure for him when creating his second album. A successful first album would push the benchmark too high for him, making the second album to be perceived as a failure.

Joe-Joe received a phone call from his mother that evening.

"Hey baby, how's the new apartment?" his mother asked.

"It's fine Ma," Joe-Joe said. "It's quiet out here, but it's better than..."

"Listen," his mother interrupted. "A young lady called here asking for you. She said you used to talk."

"Who's that?"

"She said her name is Lisa and you guy went to high school together," his mother said. "Do you know her?"

"Yeah," Joe-Joe said surprisingly. "It's been a while though."

"She left me her number to give to you."

"Ok."

His mother left him the number and hung up. It was a long time since he last associated with Lisa. Lisa was a girl who he liked very much, but she was never into him. She would always say how skinny he was and that she preferred guys who were muscular. Lisa was a girl who had it all in terms of her looks. She was attractive, light-skinned, thick, yet shapely with a fat ass that shakes when she walked in her heels.   Many people missed took her weave to be her real hair, but it wasn't; she just had that look. Joe-Joe remembered the days he tried so hard to get her attention while they were in high school, but failed. She was more attracted to the other guys in Marcy that sold drugs, who could buy her what she wanted, to maintain her lavish lifestyle. Joe-Joe felt his fame and rising fortune was what she was after. However, the thought of finally being able to fuck her overwhelmed him. The thought made him hard. An uncontrollable bulge in his pants gave way when he remembered his friends in the projects telling each other that she had recently had a tattoo put on her lower back. She was the image he would use when he was in bed alone playing with himself. She was too irresistible to pass up. He decided to call her.

"Hello."

"Hello, Lisa," Joe-Joe said.

"Yeah, who is this," Lisa responded.

"Joe-Joe."

"Hey, what's up," Lisa exclaimed nervously.

"Nothing, much."

"Nothing much, I see you all rich and famous now, huh?" She said. "I love the album; I never thought you would make it big. Everyone here is talking about you."

"I'm already trying to come up with rhymes for the

second album."

"So, when can we meet…when am I going to see you?"

"I'm in Queens…Cambria Heights to be exact," Joe-Joe said in a trembling voice.

"Oh, that far."

"Yeah."

"I mean when am I going to see you here?"

"At Marcy?" Joe-Joe asked.

"Yeah, where else."

"Nah, I'm over that fucking place, you know?"

"No, I don't know," Lisa said. "I was hoping you would come here to see me."

"I want to see you, Lisa, why can't you come here?"

"I don't like it out there in Queens; besides, I got a new tattoo that I want you to see?" Lisa laughed and giggled.

"Where?" Joe-Joe asked.

"On my upper thigh."

The last statement brought chills up Joe-Joe's spine.

"My mom is not home," Lisa said in a low voice. "She won't be home 'till noon, tomorrow, besides, I don't want to be home alone on a holiday."

Joe-Joe paused and didn't respond as he could feel the bulge in his pant starting to grow.

"You remembered what building I live in right?" Lisa whispered. "Matter of fact, it's on Marcy Avenue like yours."

"Yeah, I still do," Joe-Joe said as his mind raced back and forth over the idea of finally getting the chance to fuck the girl of his life. "Are you sure you don't want to come here, though. It's quiet over here; we can do dinner as well, you know."

"Marcy ain't all that bad, nigga," Lisa objected. "You acting like a bitch, I know it's the hood, but damn!"

"Yeah, I know but…"

"But what!" Lisa yelled over the phone. "Nigga you ain't afraid are you?"

"Alright, I can stop by…tonight."

"My apartment number is 2F."

"Come at 11:00 o'clock."

"Ok, bye."

"Bye."

Joe-Joe had finish eating two slices of pizza which he purchased after leaving the barber shop. He was ready to head out to see Lisa. He walked down Linden Boulevard to catch a dollar van to the J train at the subway station at Jamaica Center. Joe-Joe wore his heavy coat; it was brutally cold. The streets were quite empty, since most people had the day off, and used it to recover from the previous day of partying.

The dollar van dropped him off at the subway station and he purchased two tokens and walked down the long escalator to catch the J train. Because of the holiday schedule, the train skipped Flushing Avenue and he was forced to get off at Marcy Avenue. It was a long walk to the projects. As he walked along Marcy Avenue, his shoulders hunched forward and he shivered and clenched his teeth to keep them from chattering, his breath streaming against the freezing air. He crossed into Myrtle Avenue with a mounting feeling of fear pulsating from his gut. As he got closer to the housing units, he spotted a phone booth across the street. He decided to call Lisa to let her know he was a few minutes away.

"Hello," the voice said warily.

"Lisa," Joe-Joe said quivering as a cold breeze blow across his face. "I'm nearby; meet me at the door, alright?"

"Yeah, whatever," she said abruptly after kissing her teeth.

Joe-Joe heard a loud click and then the receiver ringing in his ear. Joe-Joe became a little confused about her uncanny behavior.

He adjusted his hood a little more to cover his face as he walked to her building. There was hardly anyone out on the streets, except for one guy that was at the other side of the block, at the corner looking side to side. Joe-Joe made it to the front door and rang the buzzer; no response. He rang again and he was let in the front door. He quickly walked up the steps to the second floor where she lived. He approached the door with caution and stopped. Why isn't she at the door, he thought. Joe-Joe knocked on the door and waited. There was no answer. He knocked again and still no answer. After waiting about a minute, he could hear the front door buzzer letting someone in and the front door then slammed back. He walked over to the staircase and saw the figure of two men. One dressed in a black leather goose bomber jacket with hiking boots and the other was clad in a light gray sheep skin winter coat and a matching hat. They slowly marched up the stairs staring at Joe-Joe.

To Joe-Joe's surprise, it was Devon.

"Ah fuck," Joe-Joe uttered faintly to himself, which hinted a sound of regret. Joe-Joe grabbed the railing, as fear rendered his legs like water. His eyes widened as he looked at Devon.

"You dumb ass nigga," Devon uttered slowly as he moved up the stairs. "Coming to fuck my girl, huh?"

Joe-Joe fought back fear as he could see the other man with Devon looking sternly at the front door, as he walked towards the bottom of the steps. He felt that tight, hot, choking feeling he felt the last time they met, returning. His entire body became stiff for a moment before he finally spoke.

"Yo wha'd up?"

"Fuck you man," Devon moved closer to him. "You move outta here without saying good bye. You cold, muthafucka. Now you want to fuck my bitch, nah son. Oh, I

173

get it, you a big time rappa now…huh, you think you can do whatever you fuckin' want."

"She called me," Joe-Joe responded.

"I don't give a fuck!"

"Why you trippin'. What… you expect me not to make moves and leave this fuckin' place. I'm supposed to say here forever with you?" Joe-Joe said.

Devon became furious from what he was hearing. "Shut the fuck up, nigga…you think you the shit now because you dropped an album…faggot ass bitch!"

"What I'm sayin'," Joe-Joe said, with an emptiness that seized him. "With all the money you two niggas are making, why don't you leave this place and do something else with your life. I mean you tall an' shit…you coulda played pro-basketball for the NY Knicks, but no, you wasted your fuckin' life with this shit you be sellin' on the street corner every fucking day."

"Fuck you bitch!" Devon didn't like what he was hearing and it showed on his face. "Fucking skinny ass muthafucka."

Joe-Joe began to walk pass Devon.

Devon lunged at him and pushed him on the steps.

"Where you think you going, nigga, I ain't done talkin'," Devon said moving forward as Joe-Joe got up on his feet. "You ain't escaping this bitch muthafucka!"

"I don't got no beef with you man," Joe-Joe exclaimed, moving slowly up a step. "Move outta my way."

Devon charged at him, striking Joe-Joe in the mouth with his fist. Joe-Joe felt the hit; he wobbled, panted, and choked with the blood that ran into his mouth and down his throat from his busted lips and a cracked tooth.

He sprinted towards Devon, pushing him against the wall, bewildering him long enough to rush towards the front door. As he made his way towards the door, the second man was waiting for him. Joe-Joe surged forward, throwing all his weight at him, while leaping, at the man's shoulder sending him flat on his back. Joe-Joe landed on him, got up, and managed to exit the door and staggered to the sidewalk holding his chin and covering his lips that was dripping blood. Joe-Joe dashed down Marcy Avenue. He ran across Park Avenue, dodging a series of speeding cars, and headed towards Myrtle Avenue leaving a trail of blood along his path. He could hear the two men running behind him.

"We gon' fuck you him up, nigga," he heard Devon yelling behind him.

Joe-Joe dashed swiftly towards the poorly lit playground, staggering and swaying on shaky legs. In a desperate attempt to evade the two men, he hid behind a trash can and tried to catch his breath as cold air rushed in and out of his lungs. He saw the two men looking around the playground, walking by each bench, making their way further into the dark playground. Joe-Joe could see a figure of a woman looking from an opened bathroom window of one of the apartments; he wanted to scream but didn't. As the two men walked closer to him, fear surfaced in his belly and he had a wild impulse to continue running, but instead lunged at Devon, striking him in the face as he passed by the trash can. The two men fought on, wildly swing punches at each other. Joe-Joe managed to land a left hook across Devon's right jaw which stunned him momentarily. Suddenly, before he could throw another punch, Joe-Joe felt a blow to the back of his head and then a blow from Devon to the left side of his face, which sent him crashing to the concrete pavement. Joe-Joe slowly crawled to his feet, but too dazed to rush at Devon who was standing in front of him. He vaguely heard a voice from behind him saying, "Knife that nigga, Dev!!!"

Joe-Joe, still weak from fighting, grabbed Devon's shoulders with his hands, for support, as Devon approached him. Joe-Joe screeched in agony as he felt a sharp metal object slice through his coat and into his abdomen. Joe-Joe immediately fell to his knees, while tears rolled from his cheeks. Devon advanced again and dealt him another blow, this time to his chest. A grimace formed on Joe-Joe's face and he grabbed his chest in great agony. He gazed briefly at the warm blood stain on the palm of his right hand. Trying not to succumb, he raised his head up and he caught a glimpse of the dark starry sky. Slowly he began to lose consciousness as his head touched the concrete floor.

CHAPTER SEVENTEEN

Marcus awoke from a deep sleep. He dreamt all night, but had trouble remembering his dream. He slowly returned to the current state in which he exists. It was just pass 9:00am and his mother was in the kitchen preparing breakfast. He had gotten in early the night before. He had spent time with Carter, whose brother hosted a New Year's Day party at their home in the Bronx. Upon returning home that evening from drinking and partying two days in a row, he had gone straight to bed after watching a short movie.

The aroma of breakfast caught his attention. He felt his stomach rumble with hunger. He rubbed his aching muscles around his neck area and strolled into the bathroom to wash up, while his mother finished preparing coffee. He exit the bathroom with towel in hand, and turned on the new television set he had purchased a few days ago.

"Man," said Marcus as he adjusted the antenna on the set. "'Dem eggs and sausage smell damn good, Ma." He walked over to the kitchen.

"Yes, and I also prepared coffee," his mother poured a hot cup in his favorite mug. "I know you'll need it from 'dem days you been out partying with god who knows what."

Marcus swallowed strips of fried eggs and pieces of sausage down his throat while he listened to the news being broadcast from the TV.

His mother froze, stared at the TV set, and listened to the

last segment of a news broadcast. "I knew a heard a commotion last night, while I was in bed I thought I would've gotten used to the nonsense that goes on outside."

"God damn it!" Marcus exclaimed. "Did you hear what he said, Ma? It's the second day of the fucking year and already something happened. Niggas don't even take a break on a fucking holiday...damn."

"Marcus, please, not in my house!"

Marcus started to say something, and it turned into a coughing spasm. He covered his mouth, and then wiped the food off of his lips. "The first homicide of the new year, and it had to occur here, at Marcy?" he said while he shook his head.

Marcus finished his plate and walked over to the living room window. Still chewing a piece of toast bread, he glanced over and saw a congregation of people who formed alongside Flushing Avenue. "Yeah, I knew it, the police cars are outside and they taped off certain areas, Ma."

"Did the reporter say somebody got shot?" his mother asked.

"I don't give a fuck; this place is getting on my nerves. Not even three days ago, they broke into someone's car at the parking lot...they stole loose change and shit, some cigarettes and two cassettes." Marcus smiled and walked back to the kitchen table and finished his coffee. "Actually, Ma, we can't complain... after all, this is the hood."

"So an unidentified man who was stabbed twice, was taken to the hospital?"

"Something like that, I heard...who knows somebody probably owed somebody money for crack."

"I'm so glad you're moving outta here in a couple of days," his mother said. "I'm so glad you got a steady job now and all."

"You know what, Ma, I think am going to go outside and

see what's going on out there."

"Okay, be careful, and dress warm…don't want you to catch no cold."

Marcus threw on his coat, scarf, ski cap and his newly purchased Jordans and headed down the stairs and out the front door. Marcus walked down Flushing Avenue and came upon a small restless crowd that was heading towards Marcy Avenue. They walked to Park Avenue where the police placed more barricades between Park & Myrtle. There was a lady wearing a headdress, and African beads around her neck, speaking loudly at the crowd of people. Her voice was being drowned out by the shuffling and the quiet conversations of people moving about, stretching their necks to see the crime sense. The mood of the crowd was one of despair mixed in with resentment.

About fifteen minutes had passed and the crowd started to swell as more and more people from the neighboring streets flooded the area. Marcus was bewildered by the sheer number of people who started to take interest and started flooding the streets. There have been many deaths that have occurred at Marcy before, but he'd never seen this much people come out for one dude. There were several people in the crowd he did not know, they were obviously from outside the area and not from the projects. He started to become more concern about the identity of who the victim was. He caught someone behind him saying something that immediately captured his attention.

"Same shit happened to Farod," the man said. "The shit is crazy, I'm tired of it."

"Farod?" Marcus whispered to himself and scratched his chin.

Marcus turned around, and looked at the man who spoke behind him. "Why did you mention Farod?" Marcus asked.

"Same shit happened to him," the man answered with

swift hand gestures and a tone of bitterness.

"I don't understand," Marcus said looking puzzled.

"Didn't you hear," the man said. "An aspiring rapper just got killed. That's what I heard on the news this morning."

"What rapper?" Marcus exclaimed. "I live here and I don't know any other rapper...except...he moved."

A young lady wearing skin tight jeans and a half pint jacket entered the conversation. "Isn't he the one that dropped an album the other day; what's his name?" The young lady put her right hand over her head.

"Joe-Joe," someone yelled. "I bought his album the other day too, shit was dope."

"Oh, yeah, Joe-Joe," the young lady recalled.

Marcus felt his blood boil; he almost fainted! Trying to catch his breath and his balance, he turned to the young lady and he hesitantly inquired, "Are you fucking sure the person's name is Joe-Joe?"

"People on the news were saying he was a conscious rapper," the young lady said with teary eyes. "I remember them saying he was from Marcy, too. I just got here; I live like two blocks down. When I heard it on the news, I ran out...shit is crazy."

People among the crowd could be seen wiping tears from their eyes. People had already started to whisper about the identity of the victim. Some people among the crowd admitted that they really didn't know him that much, and that his success came fairly quickly for them.

Marcus, still in complete shock, pushed his way through the crowd and ran back to his apartment. He stopped abruptly near the corner of Flushing Avenue, leaned over and vomited near a parked car. When he got inside the apartment his mother quickly approached him.

"Marcus," she said. "A man called here just a while ago,

said his name is Derek.   He said to call him as soon as possible."

"Okay," Marcus shouted back at his mother.

"What wrong," she asked. "What happening outside with all the people."

"Nothing, Ma."

"What do you mean nothing…who died?"

"Some rapper, mom."

"Okay, fine, I'm heading out to the hair dresser and pick up some groceries later," his mother said as she walked out the door.

Marcus took off his sneakers and sat on the sofa. He could not believe what had transpired. Disbelief engulfed him; he felt a pain in his belly. He couldn't bear to pick up the phone and call Joe-Joe's apartment because he knew Joe-Joe would have called him, since his story is all in the news at the moment. Overpowered by an intense sentiment of horror, unaccountable yet unendurable, he grabs a bottle of old wine stored in a shelf above the stove, in the kitchen; he proceeds to drink and endeavored to arouse himself from the pitiable condition into which he had deeply fallen into, by pacing rapidly to and from, throughout the apartment. With a growing feeling of frustration and hopeless depression, he continued to pace around the apartment searching for an answer that required a deep-rooted source. It dawned on him that he had finished the half bottle of wine and was starting to feel a little numb and light headed. He collapsed on the sofa, placed his hands over his eyes and proceeded to cry. He felt empty and void. He felt like his world was beginning to crumple around him, but from within.

A few hours had passed. The phone rang several times while Marcus lay on the couch bewildered, furious, and baffled. It rang so many times that he could not take the ring sound anymore and decided to answer it.

"Hello," Marcus answered dejectedly.

"Yo, man," Derek said with great emotion. "Where have you been, I've been trying to reach you all day."

"I'm sorry, man," Marcus heard himself saying.

"You sound like shit, I'm sure you heard what happened."

Marcus sighed and waited for his friend to speak.

"The shit is fucked up!" Derek continued. "I don't understand, he was instructed not to go back to Marcy, right...what the fuck he went there for...shit, man."

"I warned the nigga, but he didn't listen," Marcus wiped tears from his eyes. "We gotta fine out who did this shit."

"I understand, but we have to be careful the police are still investigating us and watching us, we don't need any more addition pressure right now."

"This ain't about you, it's about me," Marcus replied emphatically.

"Have you spoken to Joe-Joe's mom?"

"No."

"You need to speak to her, and see if you can get any information."

"I not sure if she's home."

"Nah, I saw her on the news...I think they are planning some kind of candle light vigil and shit around your neck of the woods there."

"Oh, yeah?"

"Some lady, an activist contacted me and wants me to speak at the event, too," Derek said.

"Yeah?"

"Yeah, and I want you and Carter to be there; it's tomorrow night."

"I guess," Marcus said nonchalantly.

"I spoke to Carter, and he feels just as bad as we do."

"So, what's goin' happen to the label?"

Derek sighed deeply. "We'll just collect on the sale of the album and his mother will get his share."

"That's not what I mean," Marcus cried.

"I don't know, man, it's hard to say right now...I guess we can search for another artist when the dust settles."

"I know but," Marcus interjected. "I don't want to be a part of the label anymore, just give me my share and I'm out."

"Fair enough."

"Joe-Joe is the second rapper that got kill here in less than a year," Marcus placed his hand over his forehead. "He was like a son to me, and look what happened."

"I know; it's a fucking shame."

Marcus could be heard sighing over the phone.

"Listen man, get some sleep and try to speak to Joe-Joe's mother."

"Yeah," Marcus said and hung up the phone.

Marcus decided he would speak to Joe-Joe's mother in the morning.

His mother had arrived home, though. She talked about the events and the people that were still outside seeking justice. Marcus ate some food his mother brought home from the Chinese kitchen a few blocks down. He went to sleep and thought about the events to take place the next day.

That night he tumbled and tossed, and could scarcely get a wink of sleep for the thoughts that were bewildering his brain. He rose with a pain in the back of his neck. He remembered dreaming, though. Marcus ribbed his eyes, as he desperately tried to remember the dream. As he recalled the dream to himself, he remembered seeing a barrel at the end of a dark tunnel. The barrel, however, was luminous, and it was the only light at the end of the tunnel. He ran towards the barrel and looked inside; he saw someone wearing a dark gray hoodie and dark blue jean looking up at him. It was Joe-Joe near the bottom, trying to climb out. There were other people climbing the walls of the barrel as well, but he could not make out who they were. Some of the people were falling from the walls of the barrel as others tried to pull them down by grabbing their ankle. The depth of the barrel appeared to have no end in sight; it was deeper than it looked on the outside sitting on the ground. He stretched his arms and tried to reach out to grab Joe-Joe who was climbing the side of the barrel, but managed to slip and fell into what appeared to be an abyss. Marcus lost memory of what had occurred after he fell.

He walked to the kitchen and prepared breakfast as usual. His mother hadn't woken up as yet, and he had the kitchen to himself. He prepared breakfast and ate. He tried not to focus too much on what had occurred the night before, but his attempts fell short; it was stuck in his mind like a nail stuck in cement. He turned on the TV and sat on the couch. The news was talking about the killing of Joe-Joe. It reported that Joe-Joe's mother had spoken to police investigators about her son's death. After an hour or so, Marcus decided he needed to visit Joe-Joe's mother before going to the candlelight vigil scheduled for later in the evening.

Marcus arrived at Joe-Joe's old apartment, to find his mother in complete despair. She stood at the front door and could barely talk but was willing to shed some light on what happened. She was dressed in her night gown, with uncombed hair sticking out on every side of her head.

"I don't know what to say, Marcus," she said in a suppressed and melancholy voice. "I don't know what he was doing here that night. Last I spoke to him he was in Queens. I was shocked when a neighbor knock on my door and told me people recognized the boy when they saw him lying on the floor with his coat soaked in blood. I was in bed at the time when I heard the knocks. I later went to the hospital and identified the body."

"Was the police there, too," Marcus asked.

"Yes, they asked me a few questions," she said clearing her throat and drying her eyes.

"Like what?"

"Did he have any reason to come to Brooklyn that day," Joe-Joe's mother said clearing her throat again. "I said not that I know of. I did mention that a young lady call me and was asking for Joe-Joe, she gave me her number and I called Joseph and told him."

"What young lady," Marcus said putting his hands in his pocket. "Do you know this woman?"

"Yes, she lives here at Marcy. She was someone that Joe-Joe had liked at one time, but she never had any interested in him...is what he told me a few years ago."

"What's her name?"

She put her head down and looked to the floor. "Lisa, she lives in one of the buildings here...I think it's the one next to this one."

"I believe I may know her," Marcus said stroking his chin.

"You know there's going to be a candlelight vigil tonight, right?"

"Yes," she said. "I'm going."

Marcus pulled away from the front of the door to signal that he was leaving.

"Marcus," she said. "Do you think this had anything to do with him being a rapper?"

"I don't know yet, but success do produce its haters."

"That's why I didn't want him to get involved in that kinda stuff."

"That has nothing to do with it," Marcus exclaimed. "Don't you hear about people in New York getting killed all the time and they're not rappers."

"I know."

"I have a couple of things I need to take care of, and I will see you at the vigil."

Marcus departed.

CHAPTER EIGHTEEN

Marcus peered through his living room window and could see the mounting crowd of people walking pass to attend the vigil outside on Marcy Avenue. He threw on his coat, scarf, jeans, and sneakers and headed outside the building. The sun had waned and already a touch of darkness was in the sky. It was growing rapidly colder and an icy wind swept through the streets of Brooklyn, New York. The streets were packed, and people were willing to brace the frigid weather to pay homage to Joe-Joe. There were a section of people, holding lit candles, who were chanting, *"No More Violence, No More Violence!"* Members of the NYPD were directing the crowd, while news reporters were out with their TV cameras interviewing random attendees and filming the event.

Marcus met and greeted Derek and Joe-Joe's mother who were amongst the angry, yet tractable crowd. A community organizer and one of the planners of the event approached and directed the three to the playground where a makeshift memorial was assembled in Joe-Joe's honor. It was in front of a tree near where the body was discovered. A yellow ribbon was placed around the trunk of the tree. A circle of religious candles, flicking in the wind, burnt at the foot of the tree, laminating the area. Flowers of all different kind, roses and carnations, were played ritualistically among the other articles. The group was awed by the sight of it despite the grief that it aroused in them. The community organizer placed a flower in the hands of the tearful mother who place it among the flowers in front of her. The group walked over to a makeshift stage in the playground, where a lady holding a megaphone, was leading the crowd in a chorus of chants. She was ferocious and her arm flung out in front of the crowd in wild protest. The three climbed up on the stage and Joe-Joe's mother was handed the megaphone and told to make a statement.

"Thank you all for coming out," Joe-Joe's mother said adjusting her scarf to block the cold wind that was battering her neck. "My son did not deserve this. He did not deserve to die. Why? Why? I want answers!" She wiped a tear drop from her right eye and continued. "Please, we need to stop the killing here. I lost a son and a daughter here…when is it going to stop!!!" She clenched her fist and shook in front of the crowd, who reacted with cheers of anger. "Enough!" She became too emotional to continue and handed the megaphone to Derek who stepped forward and spoke.

"My name is Derek Sanders…I am the president and CEO of Dynasty Records. I'm here with my colleague on my left, Marcus Carlton. We signed Joe-Joe to our label with hopes that he would produce a successful album and he did that. With your help we sold over 10,000 copies in four days so far. Joe-Joe did what many here have failed to do." Derek paused while he adjusted the volume on the megaphone. "The reason why the youth love Joe-Joe so much is because he represented hope. No matter what your situation is in life, you can escape it if you believe in yourself and work hard. Let me say this…please listen." Derek gestured with his arm to get the crowd's attention. "Being born in the projects is not a choice…but remaining in the projects is a choice." Derek paused while everyone clapped profusely. "Joe-Joe made a choice, and it was destroyed by niggas who live here…niggas who ain't got nothin' better to do but sell crack that the government dumps into our community to keep us destabilized. Joe-Joe may have died, but his music will never die." Derek waited until the crowd quieted down. "Let me say this…when we find the person who killed Joe-Joe, and we will, I can assure you, they'll be one less nigga out here selling dope."

"Justice, we need justice!" someone yelled from the crowd as Derek handed the megaphone back to the lady behind him.

The great vigil ended and everyone left. Derek and Marcus had agreed to meet again the next afternoon to get more information on Joe-Joe's killers. Marcus had told Derek what Joe-Joe's mother had told him about Lisa's involvement, earlier before the vigil. They planned to go to her apartment the next day and speak to her.

A young lady opened the door to her apartment. She was nervous and withdrawn. Marcus couldn't help but notice her beauty…her shapely figure. He stared at her hips as they expanded in the skirt she was wearing.

"Are you Lisa?" Derek asked.

"Yes."

"I hope we didn't disturb you," Derek said to her. "This is Marcus, he lives here, and we are friends of Joe-Joe."

"What do you guys want?" She asked with an attitude that made Marcus displease.

"We would like to talk to you about Joe-Joe," Derek said gently clearing his throat. "Did you attend the vigil last night?"

"No, I was busy."

"That's fine. Well, I spoke with Joe-Joe's mother and she told me that you spoke to Joe-Joe on the day he was killed. Is that correct?"

"Yeah, so, I don't got shit do with it, so why come here."

"Can you elaborate, please," Derek started to become

annoyed by her attitude. He felt the young lady was toying with him and becoming difficult. "Can you tell me the nature of the call and why Joe-Joe came back to Marcy that night?"

"How the fuck I know," she exclaimed.

"Sista, we are trying to find out what happened to Joe-Joe and who killed him."

"You know what happened," Marcus interjected. "We're going to find out the truth anyway."

"You may not know who I am," Derek spoke emphatically. "But I can tell you when we find out who killed our rapper, I can tell you that nigga won't be on the streets selling crack."

"He called me and said he wanted to meet up."

"But his mother said you called her to give Joe-Joe your number," Derek said.

"Yeah," Lisa stopped and looked down towards the floor trying to hold back her emotions. "He called me and I told him that I wanted to meet with him." Lisa folded her arms as she leaned against the door frame. "This guy I know said he wanted to see Joe-Joe, so he wanted me to get Joe-Joe to come out to see him."

"Did Joe-Joe know that he was going to see this guy?" Marcus asked.

"No, he didn't, he thought he was only going to see me." Lisa's mood was clearly changing. She became a little bit calm.

"Who is the guy that told you to get Joe-Joe to come here…what's his name?" Derek insisted.

"Devon."

"Devon," Marcus repeated.

"He lives here, he's always out there doing shit, you know selling crack."

"How do you know him?" Marcus asked.

"I used to fuck with him."

"I see," said Derek.

"I know this nigga," Marcus said. "I see him outside sometimes on Marcy pacing the sidewalk and looking side to side."

"I got to go," Lisa cried.

"I understand," Derek said quietly. "Do you think Devon is the one who killed him?"

"Yeah, he told he to bring him here and have him come to the door and don't answer it," Lisa said with great difficulty. Lisa wiped a tear drop from her eye.

"Did Joe-Joe knock on your door?" Marcus asked.

"Yeah, he did," Lisa said. "And I didn't answer it. Then I heard the buzzer again from outside and then I let them in."

"Who?" Derek said.

"Devon," Lisa replied.

"So, why did you do that," Marcus asked angrily. "I mean why?"

"He told me that all he was going to do was beat him up, because Joe-Joe owned him money, not kill him for god's sake," she cried as her eyes became red from constant rubbing. "If I'd know he was going to go that far...hell I would've tell the nigga no, shit. I had no beef with Joe-Joe."

The two men left, and walked down the stairs and out the door. It was still broad day light and the sun shone bright through the winter sky. They walked over to where Derek's car was parked, went inside. Derek started the engine and left it running. As Marcus sat in the passenger seat, he closed his eyes and searched for answers. He knew Joe-Joe was no longer involved in drugs and only acted as a look out at one time and may have acted as a runner, but was never deeply in the game. He sat back in the leather seat and closed his eyes, while his friend turned on the radio. He didn't want to talk about anything, he just wanted to know how a youth who had the world in front of him, end up being killed over nothing. Time passed and the inside of the car got warmer and Marcus unbuttoned his coat. They saw a guy in a leather trench coat walked up to a black Mercedes Benz that pulled up to the curb in front of them. The guy in the leather trench went to the passenger side of the car, leaned over to speak to the person inside for a few moments, grabbed a large roll of money out of his coat pocket and handed it to the man in the passenger seat. He stood up, looked in both directions and swiftly ran inside the building.

"Did you see that?" Derek said.

"Yeah," Marcus said scratching the back of his head.

"I thought you were sleeping."

"You kidding me," Marcus laughed. "Trust me I don't fall asleep in front of this place."

"That looked like about 25 Gees."

"That about a year's salary for niggas that lives here."

"Here's the thing that gets me," Derek said adjusting his seat. "With all the money that is flowing out of this fucking place and into these niggas pockets, why is it that when I drive down Flushing Avenue, Myrtle Avenue or even Nostrand Avenue, all I see is businesses owned by Koreans, Chinese, Jews, bodegas owned by Dominicans and Puerto Ricans, Arabs and anybody else but us."

Marcus smiled and chuckled.

"The shit is crazy," Derek laughed.

"If we stand out here," Marcus said. "You'll see this shit happening all day long like a factory."

"My point is," Derek turned to his friend and tapped him on his chest. "These niggas are rich, but they got no wealth."

"Have you spoken to Carter, he didn't show up at the vigil," Marcus said, changing the subject.

"No, he hasn't returned my calls," Derek said nervously.

"That's strange."

"I'll try him again, soon."

"Yeah, me too."

Marcus sat glaring at the housing units through the side window, thinking about how it decayed into what it has now become. He thought about everyone who he knew who tried to leave the place and move on to greater things, and how they always ended up being locked up or dead. He had less than two weeks to move into his new apartment, but that day couldn't come sooner.

"What's on your mind?" Derek turned to his friend.

"Well, you seem to have all the answers," Marcus answered back. "I was just thinking about Joe-Joe and how he almost escaped from Marcy. What went wrong?"

"You mean what he did wrong," Derek corrected his friend.

"He didn't do anything," Marcus seemed puzzle at his friend's remark. "It was that bastard...what's his name who killed him."

"Joe-Joe broke a cardinal rule, and he rightfully paid the price for it," Derek paused to take out a pack of cigarettes from the glove compartment. "You don't mind if I smoke do you, Marcus?"

"Just crack the windows a little bit," Marcus said becoming a little bit angry at the last remark his friend made.

Derek took out a single cigarette from the pack placed it in his mouth and lit it up with a lighter he had in the ash tray. "Fine," Derek continued, as he blew out smoke from his nostrils. "As I said, Joe-Joe broke a cardinal rule."

"What rule is that?"

"You never look back," Derek placed the cigarette to his mouth again and release a stream of smoke that escaped through the cracked window. "Joe-Joe looked back when he was instructed not to. Joe-Joe reached a point of no return when he dropped his debut album and achieved a certain level of fame and had moved to Queens earlier. At that point he had nothing to do with Marcy anymore, I mean nothing. His fame will harbor envy and iniquity among those he left behind."

"What about his mother?" Marcus inquired.

"She too."

"What?"

"Don't these niggas who sell crack have mothers?" Derek asked. "And how did they turn out?"

Marcus tried to ignore his friend's comments and asked about Lisa. "I hear what you're saying, Derek, but Lisa lured him to Marcy."

"He had no business getting with that bitch! She was no longer on his level. She is a hood rat. With his fame and potential, Joe-Joe could have gotten a better piece of pussy; not someone everybody in the hood ran up into. Her mind-set is strictly hood. In a few years she will continue her mother's legacy and have two or three kids by two or three different niggas who will all grow up to be like her or Devon."

"So, what about you, Derek, have you return to the hood since you moved?"

"Hell, no, everybody there knows who I am," Derek took a puff of the cigarette and let out a cloud of huge smoke and spoke very slowly. "What you think will happen, Marcus, if I go back there and start showing off my status and all, me being a record label executive; I become like a mirror to them niggas who ain't doing shit but breed hoes all day. I would end up forcing them to see themselves for what they really are…a loser, because we all grew up in the same environment, but I made it out and they didn't. And that's why they would kill me like they killed Joe-Joe."

"Okay," Marcus was a little baffled.

"What I mean is…we all grew up in the hood and we all had the same obstacles to deal with, right…so when they see me…I would make them look like…what's your excuse for not achieving your goals when I did."

Marcus coughed and opened the passenger door to let out some of the smoke that was trapped in the car.

"You see, every time they would see me," Derek continued. "I would remind them of their under achievements. You see the shit they be smoking?"

"You mean crack," Marcus answered.

"Yeah, it keeps them from seeing reality, you know, like Joe-Joe wrote in his track. It keeps them in heaven while they're still able to reside in hell. That's actually what the crack does…crack makes you live in both worlds at the same time…If I'm correct I believe that's what Joe-Joe was trying to convey in his album title track. You have to listen to his lyrics over and over again to remove the veil. The average nigga out here will listen to the song and will never see that and just remain as he is and go no further."

"It's like a fool's paradise," Marcus laughed softly.

"Exactly, those crack heads are trying to buy a stairway to heaven."

"Is that why the church makes so much money?" Marcus asked.

"My nigga, I think you have seen the light," Derek laughed out loud.

Marcus stroked his chin and meditated on what was being said.

"Check this out, homes," Derek said. "Just like the crack business, in order for the church to be successful, its members have to be living in hell…let's say mentally."

"What?" Marcus looked surprised.

"How do you sell someone a trip to paradise if they are already in paradise? Don't you notice you see more churches in the poorest neighborhoods?"

Derek paused for a moment after he spoke and looked at the police car that drove by, and then continued.

"Do you see five or six churches in on one block in any upscale community? No! Why…it's harder to sell that shit to them…it's easier to sell water to a man that's thirsty than one who's quenched."

Five minutes passed while the two sat in the car looking out their side windows.

"So, what are we going to do about Devon?" Marcus turned to his friend.

Derek took his last puff of the cigarette, blew out a load of smoke and threw the bud through the cracked window. "Have you seen him?"

Marcus closed his eyes and said, "No."

"He's probably not coming back to Marcy anytime soon, but then again you never know. There's mad money to be made here, so most likely he will be back very soon."

"If I see him, he's a dead man," Marcus said emphatically. "He's not going to get away from what he did."

"Be careful, though."

"I'll find him, trust me, I will find him."

Derek placed his seat belt on and extended his hand to his friend. "Look man, I got some business I got to take care of, we'll talk soon, alright?"

"Yeah, talk to you soon."

Marcus left the vehicle and walked back to the entrance of his building. He quickly scanned the area to see if Devon was about, however there were a few young men out on the sidewalk waiting for customers as usual. Business was minimal during the afternoon, but by sun down into the early morning twilight, the flow of revenue bled out of the hands of the poor.

He walked by the memorial that still burned with candles, and dried up roses and other flowers that littered the playground.

Marcus couldn't help but reflect on the playground which he remembered playing in as a child. The swings and the see saw was his favorite pass time activities. Now he sees a run down and deserted lot of childhood memories within a community abandoned by the city, left to rot by the materialization of drugs and violence. One thing he noticed that was missing from the community he remembered growing up in is children playing stick ball, playing tag, and shooting hoops in the basketball court on Nostrand, near Flushing Avenue. That reality has now been replaced by young men lost in a world plagued with crack cocaine. Children as young a thirteen can be seen being initiated into the game to replace those who have been killed or incarcerated. Unfortunately, those youth were the only source the residents of Marcy would turn to in order to deal with the internal brutality of poverty. They, the drug dealers, were the gate keepers of the world of make-believe. Marcus began to wonder if the narcotics were in fact a necessary evil, to provide the residents a means to escape dire poverty that penetrated the very core of their being since birth. This thought came to him as he thought about the lyrics from Joe-Joe's song, 'Escape from Marcy'. What would happen if all the drugs in the community would vanish over night? How would the addicts cope with the reality of their economic condition once the binders were removed? These thoughts plagued his mind like rats in an alley. He reached deep within his soul for answers, as he recalled what Derek just said, as he stood looking over the brick buildings of the less unfortunate in society.

Marcus made his way back to his apartment where his

mother was preparing dinner. She had just finished frying wings. The peas and rice was already done and cooling on the stove. The smell of burning grease stifled him a little as it circulated throughout the air. The television was playing his favorite game show.

"May have to crack the window a little bit, Ma," Marcus said opening the living room window.

"Come get your food, the rice is still warm."

"Ah, there's nothing like a hot meal on a cold day."

"How was the vigil last night?"

"Wonderful."

"A lot of people showed up?"

"Yeah," Marcus said nonchalantly.

"That's good, I'm glad you enjoyed it," his mother said. "So sorry what they did to the young man, dreams become nightmares when you live in places like this."

"Tell me about it."

"Chicken is done," his mother said reaching for the plate.

His mother laid the food out on the table. Fried chicken and rice was displayed along with boiled corn and fried plantains.

"Say grace, Marcus," his mother sternly looked at him.

"Ok."

Marcus said a short prayer, and attacked the food on the table.

"The news is on, it just started," his mother said stretching her neck to see the TV screen. "Hope they found out who killed the rapper."

Marcus was overwhelmed and preoccupied with the home cooked meal that he didn't hear what his mother was saying to him. He merely nodded his head while he devoured the flesh off of a bone of wings.

"Good God, thank you Jesus!" his mother exclaimed.

"Finally, our prayers have been answered…thank you Jesus."

Marcus blocked out the excitement his mother was displaying and grabbed a cob of corn of the dinner plate. The sweet taste of the corn captivated him and blocked his hearing.

"Marcus, Marcus," his mother yelled. "Can you believe that?"

"Believe what?" Marcus asked with a mouth full of corn and rice.

"They caught someone," she said excitedly. "They caught one of the guys who robbed that check cashing place on Nostrand."

Marcus swallowed the food in his mouth. He felt like his heart was burning, followed by a dizzy feeling in his head. Marcus gave the television his undivided attention. He was all ears as he turned his head behind him and listened to the latter part of the news broadcast, which showed a person who looked distinctly familiar.

"They said, they believe he drove the getaway car," his mother repeated. "They're questioning him."

"How do you know?"

"Aren't you paying attention, boy?"

"Now I am." Marcus still shaken and perplexed stood up and walked over to the TV set and looked closely at a man seen in handcuffs being escorted into a police car. He later saw a mug shot of the same man flashed across the TV set. Marcus was in pure disbelief and lost in thought. He had to pretend and control his behavior and not look suspicious in front of his mother who kept looking at him.

He finished his food and washed the dishes, and waited until his mother left the kitchen. It was no time for inactivity on his part; things were going to move very quickly. After his mother left the kitchen, he promptly grabbed the phone and dialed his friend's number.

"Hello."

"Did you see the news?" Marcus whispered looking at his mother's bedroom door.

"Actually he called me and left a message on my machine."

"We might have to start digging our graves soon."

"Well you can dig yours," Derek said. "I'll fight this through."

"Do you think he will talk?"

"Carter has nothing to lose, and maybe pressured into cutting a deal."

"What about us," Marcus said leaning over the kitchen counter with his eyes close and his hand over his forehead.

"If he breaks," Derek said. "They will get him to turn us in, for a plea deal, that's how it usually works."

Marcus became irritated. "First it was Joe-Joe and now this shit...fuck! Why I listen to you for."

"Because you wanted out of that fucking place, that's why."

"It was a big mistake. You said everything would be just fine."

"I can get you a lawyer."

"Nigga, I ain't worried about that...what I'm worried about is going back to prison."

"Relax; I'm going to get a lawyer for Carter."

"I'm back to where I started," said Marcus rubbing his watery eyes.

"Sorry you feel that way, but it ain't over yet, this is just an obstacle that we must overcome."

"What happened with Carter?"

"Apparently, someone recognized him on a newspaper footage photo from the New Year's Eve celebration and told the police about it. They claimed they remembered seeing him in the car that day. I remember he told me months back that he got out the car, walk somewhere to take a piss."

"How long do we have, you think?"

"Well it's already snowing and I heard about a foot or more and it's coming down fast. That could slow the investigation down about a day or two."

"Jesus, I can't believe this is happening to me."

"Hang tight, brother."

Marcus sighed. "I'm supposed to be moving out of here next week; now it seems like I'm never going to escape this bitch."

"The system is designed so that you don't escape it," Derek said.

"What are you saying?" Marcus asked, gasping for air. "I can't escape? I have to go, Derek…I have to go."

"Okay, get some sleep…I'll call you tomorrow."

CHAPTER NINETEEN

Marcus looked out his kitchen window and saw snowflakes dropping from the sky like fallen stars. The streets were covered with about a few inches of snow already and the number of cars on the roads began to diminish. Although the night was still young, he decided to retire and go to bed early, hoping to wake up from the brutal nightmare that he found himself in. After a long shower, and a cold beer, he laid his head on the pillow, rolled his warm blanket over his head and drifted into oblivion.

He woke up out of his sleep, tired and drained. He look at the clock, and to his amazement, it was only one o'clock in the morning. He got less than four hours of sleep. He went back to bed, closed his eyes and tried to force himself to sleep. After twisting and turning in the sofa, he finally gave up and walked to the refrigerator for another can of beer. No beer, no milk, and only two eggs left in the refrigerator. He slammed the door shut and cursed under his breath. Pacing back and forth, in his boxers, his emotions went from anger to doubt and back again constantly. "I need a fucking beer," he said to himself. "No, I need to escape this shit," he mumbled. Marcus looked out the living room window at the pile of snow on Flushing Avenue. Hardly a soul was on the streets. The snow covered everything; and the sight of it seemed foreign to him. Depression hit him like a bolt of lightning. He lifted his hands to his face and touched his trembling lips. The pain was too great for him to endure. The thought of going back to prison and spending the rest of his life there, and not being able to see his daughter again, sent his mind into a fiery rage that brought on small series of convulsive movements. Out of the blue, he started laughing and then moments later it metamorphoses into deep depression which brought forth tears. He went from one extreme to the next within a few seconds and this continued for several minutes. At one point he became hysterical and started laughing profusely for no apparent reason, only to feel a flash of depression afterwards.

Marcus never smoked crack in his life, but this was the first time the thought ever crossed his mind. It would be the only thing that would prevent him from losing his mind. Crack cocaine, he thought, would prevent him from seeing his current predicament. The pain and anguish became too much for him to bear, and he wrestled with his lower nature, and fought long and hard, yet he succumbed. Now he lay on the living room floor and began crawling on his belly like a lizard. Suddenly, the thought of suicide slightly crept into his psyche and left like a passing wind. He got up on his feet and reached for his pants, his boots, his sweater, and his overcoat and got dress. He dragged himself out of the house in the middle of the night. "I'm doing this for my daughter," he said out loud as he rationalized his actions.

Marcus turned off the lights, closed the apartment door and headed down the steps and into the cold snowy streets of Brooklyn, New York. He proceeded towards Marcy Avenue. He fought through the unplowed snow which was just below his knees. It was cold and windy, but he advanced forward, as the snow continued to fall from the sky, looking for someone to save him from his insanity.

He surveyed the area, looking up and down the avenue; when he got to Park Avenue he preceded towards Myrtle

Avenue. On and on he walked with no end in sight as he saw no one, until a Jeep pulled up next to the sidewalk. At a distance, he could see a man leaving the rear passenger side of the vehicle. He continued to advance to the end of the block as snowflakes started to obscure his vision. He came closer to the man on the sidewalk, and became nervous. As he came within a few feet of the man who was talking to someone in the parked vehicle, he could hear someone from the vehicle say something to the man on the sidewalk.

"Yo, Dev, check you later, man," a heavy set man in the driver side of the vehicle said as the car drive off into the snowy streets.

Marcus felt his heart skip a beat and he slightly turned his head around only to glimpse someone he recognized. It was Devon! He was wearing a black leather goose bomber jacket, a black skull cap, and a pair of Timberlands.

"Looking for a hit?" he asked Marcus who pulled his hood further over his head, covering his face, trying to avoid being seen. "I work this area," he said to Marcus as he walked by.

"Nah, I'm good," Marcus said as he continued walking through the snow.

Was it merely a coincident, or could fate be instructing him, was what came to his mind? Anger brewed within him at the sight of Devon; it made his blood boiled. Devon had something he needed badly, which created a conflict within his very soul. Not knowing what to do, he walked on towards Nostrand Avenue. His legs became tired and his feet were blistered and near frostbitten. He turned the corner and continued to struggle through the snow when all of a sudden he started to hallucinate. There was a young man up ahead standing on the sidewalk near a fire hydrant. "That nigga, must be freezing his ass off," Marcus said to himself as he notice the young man wasn't wearing a coat. All the young man was wearing was a dark grey hoodie sweater and dark blue jeans. Marcus whipped the snow off of his face and took a closer look at the uncanny figure. "Joe-Joe," he said with great awe as he walked faster towards the image. Suddenly, he tripped and fell to the ground on top of snow that broke his fall, but he was able to get up while brushing off the snow from his coat and pants. He looked straight ahead but there was no one in sight, the image he saw was gone. "Joe-Joe!" he yelled into the snowy air. He looked around and around between the parked cars covered with snow, but there was no sign of Joe-Joe. He walked over into the middle of the street looking both ways, and still no sign of him. He realized he saw what might very well have been a mirage. All of a sudden, he heard himself speaking, hoarsely, faintly to himself once again and laughing for no reason.

His impulse was dead locked; he knew what he wanted to do next. His only thought was to get back to his apartment immediately, and fast! He walked on and finally made it to the front door and walked hurriedly up the stairs to the third floor.

Snow dripped off of his boots and on to the living room floor creating a trail of water as he marched to the kitchen. He opened one of the draws and pulled out a knife with a five inch blade used for craving steak and walked over to the sofa and sat on the edge of it with his head between his knees, waiting to catch his breath.

He felt his mind slipping and becoming depraved. He had nothing to lose and nothing to gain at this point in time. It was dark in the apartment, the lights were off and his mother was still asleep with the door closed. He waited in silence for a good ten minutes, staring at the open door leading out into the staircase. He knew he was at a crossroad and a decision where there was no coming back from. Anything could happen; he knew there was a possibility he may not make it back in the apartment. He may not ever see his daughter or his mother again. He was afraid and didn't know what to expect out there. He had to go, it was no coincidence what occurred out there, he thought. Was Joe-Joe reaching out and trying to tell him something? He felt guilty for Joe-Joe's death. He felt guilty for not attending the funeral. He stood up, unbuttoned his coat, and hid the knife in an inside pocket. He walked to the kitchen again for a cup of water which he slowly drank to quench his thirst. He walked out and closed the door behind him, marched down the stairs and into the streets once again.

He took the same path he did the first time. The snow drift had picked up a little and the accumulation had increased. Devon was not in his sight. He turned right on Marcy Avenue and proceeded to where he originally saw Devon several minutes ago. There was a lady approaching him struggling through the snow with a blanket over her back as she tried to use the rest of the blanket to cover her chest. When she walked by they made eye contact. Marcus had seen the woman before in and about the housing project. She had a dead stare; there was no life in her eyes. Her face was boney and lifeless. As she walked by, Devon came into view; he was smoking a cigarette and moving about to keep warm. It was the dead of night and there was no one around; just the two of them. Marcus felt his coat to make sure his knife was still in his inside coat pocket. Devon stared at him, slightly turning his head to the left while holding a cigarette to his mouth. Fear did not escape him, as he walk up to Devon.

"Ya changed ya mind, nigga," Devon said. "It's too cold to be walking around in circles."

"I guess it's not too cold for you to be waiting out here in the middle of the night," Marcus looked at him sternly.

"Yeah," Devon replied with confidence. "But I get paid

to be out here, you don't."

"What do you know about a guy name Joe-Joe," Marcus demanded. "You know, the rapper."

"What about him?" Devon answered. "Besides, you want something from me, nigga? Keep it moving, if you ain't no customer."

Marcus cleared his throat, turned his head and look down the street and over his shoulder. "Dude, I'm ma asked you again," Marcus said in a very agitated voice. "What do you know about a rapper that lived here name Joe-Joe?"

"Fuck that nigga!" Devon exclaimed as he removed the cigarette from his mouth. "You think I give two fucks about him. Don't come here in my face with this bullshit, nigga." Devon threw his arms to the sides and took a step back. "I don't stand out here by myself, nigga; you don't know the niggas I'm down with." Devon put the cigarette to his mouth, inhaled, and blew out a stream of smoke through his nostrils. "Yo, get out of my face you fucking bitch."

"Who killed Joe-Joe," Marcus turned directly face to face with Devon. "I won't ask you again."

"You may end up like him in a minute if you don't keep it moving."

Without warning, Marcus felt a swift blow to the side of his head which knocked him to the snowy ground. It felt like a brick had hit him. The snow broke his fall and he went blank for a few seconds.

Marcus opened his eyes, stood up, looked left to right and saw Devon walking down towards Myrtle Avenue. He gave chase and followed him, walking swiftly to catch up with him. Marcus squinted, his vision blurred before coming back into focus. Devon was a few feet away from him and saw him and turned and looked at Marcus, and stopped. Devon was slightly taller and more muscular than him, but he was not going to let

Devon get the best of him, regardless of his height.

Marcus locked eye with Devon who cautiously waited for him. Marcus could hear his heart beating. His tongue was dry with excitement; he could feel the adrenaline pumping through his vein; every fiber in his body was now eager to annihilate the adversary. It was fight or flight and he was not going to back down.

Devon threw the first punch and missed and threw another, this time a left hook and completely missed Marcus' face by a few inches. The miss made him a little unbalance as his left foot slipped on the snow. Marcus took advantage of the opportunity and hit him as hard as he could and put all of his weight into the blow. Devon was shaken by the hit to the side of the head. Standing but staggering, Marcus tackled him to the snowy ground. A struggle ensued as Marcus wrestled to stay on top. With Devon's face partly covered with snow, and eyes partly open, Marcus landed a series of blows to the head and face causing blood to leak from his nose. Exhausted and out of breath, Marcus stood up and look down at his foe lying on the ground trembling while snow began to accumulate on his body. Marcus leaned down and grabbed Devon's unconscious body and turned him on his belly. Marcus unbuttoned his coat. He removed the knife he had hidden in his inside coat pocket. His hands were numb from the cold air and almost frost-bitten, but he managed to grip the handle with his right hand hard enough to hold it in place. The streets were barren except for the snow, and a hungry looking dog wondering the streets probing for food. Marcus unapologetically grabbed Devon forehead with his left hand, pulling Devon's head towards him while placing the blade of the knife under his neck as he slit his throat from ear-to-ear. He felt the warm blood touch his frost-bitten hand. Marcus looked in horror as blood spurted out and splattered on to the snow, turning it red. Marcus placed the bloody knife back in his coat pocket and buttoned his coat. He washed his hands with the snow on the ground and managed to get most of it off and staggered back down Marcy Avenue. He finally made it back to his apartment, undressed and collapsed on the couch.

Marcus was awakened by a gentle touch from his mother. Still dazed and half unconscious, he managed to focus on his mother standing over him holding a spatula. He stood up, yawned and rubbed his eyes and cleared his throat.

"Boy, I thought you'd never get up," his mother said walking back to the kitchen. "I made some pancakes for ya."

Marcus nodded and went to the bathroom to wash up. He washed his hands a lot longer than he normally does. Although there were no stains on his hands he fanatical scrubbed his hand with a bar of soap, washing it off with warm water only to suds up again with soap, rinsing it off with warm water.

"Marcus," his mother yelled from across the kitchen. "Your pancakes are getting cold."

Marcus walked to the kitchen table which had coffee and pancakes lay out on the table.

"You look a mess," his mother stared at him. "What, you been out partying all night are somethin'. That was some snow storm; I hope you didn't get caught up in it. Sorry I couldn't buy any syrup, money is tight...just use the butter I have there instead."

Marcus didn't say a word and stared at the two pancakes stacked on the plate before him. His appetite for food was lost in memory of recent events. Depressed and dejected, he managed to finish his coffee and the two pancakes which he grabbed with his fingers.

"Don't you hear the door bell, boy?" he mother asked

him.

His mother walked over to the front door and opened it. It was a neighbor on the third floor. She was a little shaken.

"Did you see the police and ambulance this morning, Dorothy," she said.

"No, what happened?"

"They found a dead body lying on the snow outside on Marcy Avenue this morning."

"Oh god, more gang violence, I supposed."

"Who knows, I heard someone saying that he was a known crack dealer around here."

"So many killings, it's not safe to walk the streets anymore. When is President Bush going to do something about the crack in the black communities? They talk about the war on drugs, but the war is on us. Well, at least we have a black man in City Hall now; hopefully things will start to change."

"Mayor Dinkins...we'll have to just wait and see."

"Change will come...I can see it."

"I got to go, Dorothy, but tell Marcus to be safe out there; it's getting worse, first the rapper and now this."

"Take care, sister."

His mother closed the door and stormed over to her son who was pouring another cup of coffee.

"Boy, did you hear that," she said. "There's been another killing, this time on Marcy Avenue."

Marcus yawned, licked the butter off of his fingers and stared into the air in front of him.

"I haven't been to church in a long time and they having a christening for that baby boy, you remember, right, Marcus, the one I'm godmother for. Well the family is coming to pick me up and I'm so glad they started to clean most of the snow already."

His mother shuffled back to her room where she grabbed her pocketbook and marched out of the apartment.

Marcus started to experience relapses of depression and is now in need of something to numb the pain. He felt lethargic and malnourish. Last night's event lingers in his mind like a fly that would not go away, no matter how much he tried to forget it. Things were never supposed to have gotten this far. It was all Derek's fault, he considered. If he only had said no when they were at the bridge that day, he would be in a better position in his life. Now the thought of committing murder a second time have left a throbbing pain in his belly.

Marcus placed his hands over his ears; he could hear the crack cocaine calling him from within. It was the only way out of his anguish. He was in a desperate situation and would make another attempt and seek out the neighborhood for a crack dealer.

He decided to give Derek a call; he needed the reassurance from him. He picked up the phone and dialed his number, it kept ringing, but no one answered. He slammed the phone down almost breaking it, to his disappointment.

Marcus grabbed his coat and the rest of his clothes and left to walk the streets of Brooklyn. The cold air hit him hard in the face, causing him to tilt his head down to avoid the full impact. He walked slowly towards Marcy Avenue and witness a few police cars and plain clothes police officers scouting the area. He wanted to turn around but didn't want to seem suspicious; instead he walked a couple of feet, stopped and pretended like he forgot his keys by touching his pockets and turned around and walked towards Nostrand Avenue.

There was still fresh snow on the sidewalks. The main roads were being plowed by trucks and a few people were seen shoveling and cleaning snow off their vehicles. One thing that was missing was children from the projects playing snow ball fight. Now that word has gotten around that someone was killed in the projects, that reality would never come forth.

There was no one in sight; that is, no one selling crack. The police presence seemed to have frightened all the dealers away, at least temporarily. "When I would never consider taking that shit, everybody would be out here like roaches, now that I desperately want it, not a nigga in sight," he whispered sternly under his breath. He walked long and hard, shuffling his feet through the fresh snow, from Myrtle Avenue to Bedford Avenue and to Broadway.

CHAPTER TWENTY

Marcus never believed the day would ever come that he would find himself searching the streets of Brooklyn for crack. He had lost the battle, and realized who his greatest enemy is. He had survived thirteen years of hard times at a penitentiary, but couldn't make it out of Marcy. Everything was falling apart like a broken house made of limp worthless cards. He found himself walking around in circles. Two hours had pass since he left the projects. The journey seemed endless with no resolution in sight. He began laughing loudly to himself for no reason and hid his face from any onlookers who he caught staring at him.

He began to worry that he may lose his mind at any moment; it was becoming more and more depraved as the urge to kill in order to stay alive became more present in him. He killed twice already since returning to Marcy, and he no longer felt any guilt for doing it. He needed a hit bad in order to maintain some level of mental stability and morality.

Marcus continued to walk on Broadway. The streets were plowed and most of the storefronts were already clean. Momentarily, he wept, he began to feel pain in his knees. He continued walking not knowing where he was going at this point. Up ahead he could hear voices, people singing, and praising. He walked a few stores down to where the noise was coming from. It was a church, a small one. It sat next to a furniture store and a nail salon. He saw a congregation of a few people sitting in pews. There was a small choir singing. The music brought a sense of comfort to him and a piece of mind. A woman in her forties saw him through the glass window of the church and quietly walked up to him, as he looked in from the sidewalk. She opened the front door, smiled and peacefully approached him. She had a dark complexion, and wore a red broad hat on her head; she was neatly dressed and soft spoken.

"Excuse me, sir," she said while holding on to the open door. "Would you like to come in from the cold?"

Marcus twitched his head and looked over at her holding the door open for him. "I'm looking for something," Marcus mumbled, a normal frightened look in his eyes now.

"You may find it here," the lady said to him. "You look troubled, come on in." She pointed to the entrance that led to the open congregation.

Marcus awkwardly removed his hood and nervously walked in. The lady showed him an empty seat near the rear of the church; three rows from the back. Marcus searched the room with his eyes. It was an open space, with a small band which consisted of a drummer, a guitarist, and a keyboard player. A bearded man wearing a purple robe sat on the balcony with another man about arm's length away.

"Have a seat," the lady said, lightly touching him on his shoulder.

The choir continued singing a hymn that Marcus remembered his grandmother singing as a child. When the chorus ended and a young lady got up from the first row and spoke a few words and introduced the pastor of the church.

The pastor was an overweight man and carried a deep voice that echoed through the microphone speakers. About ten minutes through his sermon, the congregation became electrified and began shouting and praising while the band played. Women got up on their feet and cheered waving their hands and dancing in the aisles. The pastor's speech became emotional and poignant. He talked about how Lazarus was persecuted only to be raised from the dead. The pastor was given a towel and a glass of water half way through. Marcus felt uncomfortable and out of place. It was the first time since he was a child, that he been inside of a church.

The pastor carried on preaching, invoking the congregation of mostly women and children, into a frenzy. He lifted his eyes over the heads of the worshippers, with arms outstretched and powerful hands gripping the pulpit, his deep voice roared forth like a lion in the wilderness. As he concluded his sermon he called over the man who was sitting next to him earlier and whispered something in his ear. The man stepped down from the rostrum and walked over towards Marcus.

"Hi I'm Deacon Moore, the pastor would like for you to come forward to the podium," he said quietly.

Marcus stood up and the deacon guided him to the front of the rostrum facing the pastor.

"We have a gentleman here with us today who came in from the streets to visit us," the pastor said closing his bible. "I never met him before, but the Holy Ghost is telling me that this man is in trouble."

Marcus looked up at the pastor and nodded while holding his hands behind his back.

"The Lord has brought you here," said the pastor with outstretched hands. "It is time for you to ask for forgiveness for your transgressions."

Marcus tried to speak, to answer but something within him knew that there was no turning back from what occurred last night in the snow storm. He moved his mouth but nothing came out, his heart was heavy with grief, his eyes teary.

"Confess!" the pastor exclaimed through the microphone as he stepped down from the podium holding the microphone in his hand. "The lord wants to save you, but you must first confess to him. The spirit tells me that there is something that you need to get off your chest...so the lord may enter. Tell the church why you came here, my brother." The pastor places the microphone to Marcus' mouth.

"I...I committed a great sin," Marcus mumbled into the microphone placed before him. "I killed a man; last night...I slit his throat."

A quiet commotion could be heard amongst the congregation. One lady, wearing a red dress and a black hat, got up out of her seat and waved her hand in the air and rocked back and forth looking upward towards the ceiling. "Hallelujah," she said. "Praise be the glory." She sat back down in her seat.

Marcus lowered his head in shame, arched his back. "I robbed a store and killed a woman for money a few months ago at a check cashing place not too far from here," Marcus continued wiping tears from his eyes. "I have nowhere to go."

The lady in the red dress got up out of her seat again waving her hand and began speaking in tongues. "Shaalaabaa...Blood!" she exclaimed. "More blood shaabaa...will shed before death cometh to you...Hallelujah Zephaniah...the angel of death walks with you my brotha...I see more blood on the streets of Brooklyn...Hallelujah praise God...the angel of death is guiding you...Hallelujah."

The pastor, stunned and bewildered, cleared his throat, looked at the congregation wild-eyed and passed his hand over his head from front to back while the lady in red continued to speak in tongues. "The Holy Spirit is with us, it is speaking through her," he said pointing at the lady in red. "Where did you kill this man?" the pastor asked Marcus methodically.

"Marcy...I live in the hood."

"I see," said the pastor who beckoned to the deacon by tilting his head. "You may leave here in peace. I wish you well."

The deacon grabbed Marcus by the arm and led him down the aisle as church goers covered their mouths in astonishment. Marcus could hear the lady in red prophesying about his destiny in the background as he continued to walk. He reluctantly was led out the front door and into the snow covered streets.

Marcus was shaken by the recent event. Troubled by what he heard coming from the church, he began to wonder whether or not he might in fact be battling fate. Was his destiny already written out for him from the beginning, he asked himself while crossing the street? He thought about growing up in the hood, and how others more fortunate than him could be given opportunities in a more pleasant environment without having to deal with the trials of others less fortunate. Why couldn't he have been born somewhere else? He remembered what Derek told him in his car.

Marcus nearly slipped on a patch of frozen ice, catching his fall as his hands touched the ground. At that moment he realized that he still had his bloody knife in his coat pocket from last night. He was shocked that the knife was still in his coat pocket; he taught he removed it. He kept his hood over his face, his head down and kept walking.

He walked in front of a Spanish bodega and was captivated by the aroma of fresh coffee brewing from the machine. When he walked in, there was only a young black woman and her infant son and a Spanish lady behind the counter.

Marcus helped himself to a cup of coffee.

"That shit is fuckin' crazy," the Spanish lady said. "What

the fuck is this!"

Marcus turned around and saw that they were watching a TV screen that hung from the ceiling near the front of the store. Marcus listened to the broadcast while he prepared his coffee, pouring sugar and milk into a paper cup filled with black coffee.

"*...he was shot twice, once in the shoulders and once in the head by NYPD detectives who arrived at his Fort Greene apartment to issue an arrest warrant for the murder and robbery of two owners of a check cashing establishment in the Bedford Stuyvesant section of Brooklyn back in the late summer. He was shot when he tried to prevent police from entering his apartment. Police recovered from his body the same gun used in the brutal killing.*" The announcement ended for commercial break.

Marcus froze and could not believe what he heard. His tongue became extremely dry and his legs stiff. The young woman with the baby placed two cartons of milk on the counter and spoke.

"I heard they lookin' for the other muthafucka who was there too," she said. "The police are all over Marcy right now looking for his ass."

"Wasn't there a stabbing there last night during the storm?" the Spanish woman asked excitedly as she covered her forehead with her hand. "That shit is crazy."

"You know, he was the head of Dynasty Records, too," the black woman said. "He produced Joe-Joe's album, remember?"

"The guy the police shot, right?"

"Well actually both of them were down with Joe-Joe."

He watched the two women preoccupied with their conversation and slowly walked out of the store with the cup of coffee in hand undetected.

He became very nervous; his hands began to shake uncontrollably. He realized that his fate was sealed; they were looking for him now.   Blood was about to be spilled on the streets since he would do anything to see his daughter, he thought to himself, as the lady in the church said. He had hardly realized the news, further than to understand that he had been brought in on one moment face to face with something unexpected and final. He could never return home again. He had to make two phone calls. He needed to speak to his daughter, but he also had to try and call his mother too.

The bitter cold started to take a toll on him. His legs still hurt and his whole body was shivering as the cold wind pick up as the night approached. The hot coffee helped a bit, but the effects where momentary.

He walked to a pay phone at the corner of the block. He pulled out a quarter from his pocket and stared at the phone for a moment and dialed.

"Hello."

Marcus could hear the despair in his mother's voice.

"Hello, Hello," she said.

Her voice wasn't the same. It was void of life, void of energy, and void of hope. She stopped saying "Hello" and then there was a long silent pause. He could feel his mother crying silently on the other end. The fact that she didn't hang up meant she knew who was on the other end of the phone. It was very painful for him, he wept.

Marcus tilted his head forward and whispered, "I love you Mom," and placed the phone on the receiver. He knew the next call was going to be very different. He searched his pocket and found two dimes and a nickel. He placed them into the phone slot and dialed this daughter's mother's phone number. It rang and someone picked up.

"Hello."

Marcus paused for a few seconds and said, "Hello Keisha."

"Dad, is that you," she said in awe. "Where are you?"

"Keisha," he said. "Where's your mother?"

"In the shower…but dad…you're on TV."

"Good, listen to me," he interrupted. "Everything you hear about me on the news is true. Honey, your father made a lot of bad decisions…and I'm paying for it now."

"Am I going to see you," she said as her voice became more tearful. "What's happening."

"I'm sorry honey, I'm so sorry…I was only trying to get myself out of a situation and I just fucked up badly…I'm sorry."

"No…I want to see you."

"You can't honey…and you know why."

"No…"

Marcus remained silent as he tried to contain himself for a moment. He had to stay strong for his daughter.

"I can come see you and they won't know…please," she pleaded. "Where are you…please."

"Don't cry honey…Daddy loves you."

"No…you don't," she said angrily. "Why can't I see you?"

"Ok," he said clearing his throat and looking over his shoulders. "You can meet me tonight, then." He sighed and continued. "Meet me in Williamsburg on Montrose Ave and Lorimer Street…if you don't see me there go in the park there I think it's called Sternberg Park."

"Ok…daddy."

"And do me a favor, don't tell anyone and I mean anyone where you're going, including your mother. And if anything happens, tell her I love her…you hear sweetie?"

"Okay."

"It's getting dark and I won't have to hide much. Try to be here by 7:30."

"Okay, daddy."

"Be careful and dress warm."

"Bye, I love you."

Marcus hung up the phone and looked around the neighborhood and started walking in circles. The hardest thing was talking to his daughter. He knew the situation he was in; it was dire and critical. He did not want his daughter to be a part of it.

Suddenly, his heart skipped a beat; a police car had just turned the corner up ahead at the corner of the block. He managed to slip into a nearby laundry mat and hid behind a video game machine before the car even finish making the turn. He watched as the police car drove by. There were two police officers in it, looking apprehensively at every car and person walking the sidewalk. Marcus imagined that most people in the neighborhood didn't know too much about what was going on and his identity maybe fairly safe. The police car passed through into the next block and down the street. He had to walk in circles to kill time. He walked around Williamsburg endlessly not knowing where fate would lead him. There were mostly Jewish stores and Jews everywhere and a few sanitation trucks removing the snow off the streets. He was getting hungry and figured he would wait until his daughter arrived and then he would have her buy something for the two of them.

Marcus found himself close to the Brooklyn Queens Express and felt he was too far from where he had to be to meet his daughter. His knees were becoming stiff and tired but he kept walking. He turned and headed back when he noticed his picture on a poster stapled to a telephone pole. He was astonished and baffled. He only noticed it because he looked up. The only thing that saved him was the fact that most people in the neighborhood were paying no attention. As

221

he walked down the next block he saw another poster with his picture on it, they were everywhere!

The streets were getting dark and he would slow his pace a little. Unexpectedly, the thought came to him that maybe he could escape to New Jersey and live under a false identity. It was just a thought and it escaped his mind quickly as it entered it. He came upon a quiet and lonely block and he would rest his legs a bit on a bench next to a parking lot. It was the first time in hours that he was able to rest.

About fifteen minutes passed and he got up and started walking again this time to the park to meet his beloved daughter.

He saw a middle aged woman with long leather boots and a short leather trench coat with the front opened up walking towards him with two shopping bags. Trying to avoid the snow she left and walked off the sidewalk and over onto the street where the streets were already cleaned. They glanced at each other, and she did a double take and turned her head again and looked directly into his eyes and blushed.

Marcus saw horror and fear in her eyes! That was not the look of seeing a black man at night look, which he is used to seeing. This was a different kind of look! He felt a keen sensation of numbness flush over all his skin. His heart raced. He didn't feel anymore tiredness in his legs. The adrenaline was pumping and he could feel it all over his body as he continued to walk. He turned at the corner of the block and stopped and hid behind a tree. She couldn't see him. She was very nervous, he noticed. She went to a parked car and opened it and placed her shopping bags in it. Surprisingly, she didn't get in. Instead she closed the door and ran across the street. Her gait was very irregular. Marcus wondered why she didn't just drive off, and where was she going. He noticed that she was heading for the phone booth across the street and stopped in front of it.

"Fuck!" Marcus yelled quietly. "Don't do it, bitch...don't do it!"

Marcus unbuttoned his coat and walked halfway across the street and stopped to let a car that was driving by, pass in front of him. The woman was frantically searching for change in her purse, when he discreetly walked over to her. He waited momentarily for another car to drive by as he stood behind her. There was no stop sign on the road. He reached into his coat pocket and touched the handle of the knife with his hand and pulled it out slowly. Still not noticing him, she placed a coin in the slot and removed a piece of hair from her face. Before she could dial a digit, he grabbed her by the hair and pulled it back exposing her thin neck that displayed a six pointed star attached to a gold chain and thrust the blade of the knife into her throat. The knife didn't go deep enough and she gasps for air causing blood to shoot out of the hole in her throat as she exhaled. She managed to scratch him on the side of his face as she fell to her knees. Still holding on to her hair from the back of her head, he held the knife tighter this time, with the blade and his hands dripping with blood. She tried helplessly to break his grip as her instinct for survival kicked in. He bent his knees slightly, lowered his back and pulled his arm back and thrust another blow of the knife deep into her throat hitting the neck bone.

An orgasm of rage and social resentment suddenly came over him; he thrust the knife into her throat again and again repeatedly. He felt the adrenaline pulsating harder and harder into his vein with each thrust of the knife. Blood flowed from her throat down her chest and over her pink breasts. He released his grip and wiped his face with the sleeve of his coat to remove the trickle of blood that splattered on his face. He stepped back and looked at the pool of blood that formed on the thin layer of snow covered ground, turning it dark red, as her body lay lump and lifeless. He dropped the blood covered knife and left it at the scene.

A car drove by and slowed down, as he walked away from the scene, the car quickly drive off causing the tires to screech against the pavement. The vehicle made a quick left turn and double parked in front of a restaurant. Marcus could see the driver of the vehicle running out of his car and into the restaurant colliding with a patron, as he ran down the street wiping the blood off his hands on the bottom of his coat.

Marcus continued to run; nowhere in particular, but he was heading west. He wasn't afraid anymore; he knew fear was useless at this point. He no longer chose to fight but to flee; he had reached the end of his rope and there was nothing left to fight for. He knew he would never be able to be there for his daughter or his mother. He was alone, homeless and the most wanted man in New York City. Nothing could save him now; the choice he had was life in prison or death, and it wasn't much of a choice.

He could hear sirens in the distance behind him. He turned and saw flashing lights and made a quick turn and ran to Grand Street and rested for a few minutes. His knees trembled, his feet was bruised and blistered, his arms hung limp from his shoulders, his back ached, and his eyes burned. He was very hungry. He walked over and rested on the steps of a local synagogue to catch his breath and to collect his thoughts. He covered his face with his hands and rested his elbows on his knees. He was now facing triple murder, and life in a maximum security state prison. That predicament would be worse than death, he thought. He searched for hope and said a short prayer as his eyes filled with tears.

"Oh God, please have mercy on me," he said timidly to himself. "Help me out of this for once...please. All I wanted was an opportunity…a second chance. Please, help me. Guide my daughter and secure her future as I walk through the valley of the shadow of death."

A car drove by, and he immediately braced himself to start running, but he noticed it wasn't a police car. He got up, looked around and started walking down Grand Street. It was fairly empty and quiet except for a few Orthodox Jews who walked passed him. He continued to walk. He knew the police were looking for him in the area. He felt they were closing in on him; he could hear the sirens moving closer.

His eyes bulged; he could see the Williamsburg Bridge up ahead. A feeling of relief overshadowed his entire body when he saw something of majestic proportions; it was the Twin Towers. They came into view from behind the bridge; he almost felt he was already in the big city. He quickened his pace and headed for the entrance to the bridge. On the other side was Manhattan.

"I could find a phone booth in Grand Central and call my daughter and have her meet me there instead," he whispered to himself.

He made his way passed the entrance and took another glimpse at the Twin Towers.

There was still a few inches of snow left on the pathway of the bridge; it would slow him down a bit, but it was not a discouragement to make the half a mile run.

Suddenly, Marcus heard a car pulling up behind him with flashing lights.

"Freeze…remove your hood, turn around and let me see your hands," a voice yelled from behind him.

He slightly turned his head and ran as fast as he could, out running the police officers, who left their patrol cars and ran after him. He could feel his heart pounding in his chest like a drum as he made it almost half way across the bridge only to see officers from the other side running towards him.

"Stop, put your hands up," an officer exclaimed, pointing a gun at him.

Marcus stopped and looked at the officers running after him from both sides of the bridge, with guns drawn and flash lights in hand. Anxious and frightened, he immediately started climbing up until he got to the top of the fence, looked over at the skyscrapers across the East River and climbed over the top. He could see and hear screams, yells and lights flashing from opposite sides of the bridge. He managed to climb over the fence and to the other side; he slipped and landed on the narrow ledge below that barely had room for his feet. He looked down below his feet and saw a small tugboat passing under the bridge.

The officers all gathered around him on the other side of the fence, frozen and staring at him in complete shock. Marcus looked up at the sky, held his breath, said a short prayer and released his fingers from the fence. He felt his body falling with the wind against his back. He opened his eyes and saw a configuration of stars twinkling in the dark ocean above while he felt his body crashing against the cold dark ocean below. He felt ice cold water all around him, rushing into his nostrils and into his lungs; it stifled him. A bright light appeared in his mind momentarily and turned to complete darkness shortly thereafter. There was darkness everywhere and he ceased to know.

ABOUT THE AUTHOR

This is the debut novel of Leon Thomas. He currently works in the legal field and chooses writing as a hobby. He lives in Queens, New York and is a graduate of St. John's University. The author can be reached at email:
LThomas1128@hotmail.com